MARGERIE'S TURN

EPISODES IN A LIFE

by Brent Isgrig

Publishing Coordinator – Sharon Kizziah-Holmes

Paperback-Press
an imprint of A & S Publishing
A & S Holmes, Inc.

ISBN -13: 978-1-956806-30-4

ACKNOWLEDGEMENTS

The encouragement and support of The Lost Star in Paris, France, and thoughtful input from Sally Engel, are deeply appreciated. Sharon Kizziah-Holmes, astute publisher of Paperback Books, was helpful in every way.

For three remarkable decades I was surrounded by creative, diverse, outspoken, and fascinating people. The place, the period, and surprises, helped a young man discover the meaning of joy and character. So thank you New York City for being all that you were; this book is a tribute to you.

For man, the vast marvel is to be alive. For man, as the flower and beast and bird, the supreme triumph is to be most vividly, most perfectly alive.

Whatever the unborn and the dead may know, they cannot know the marvel of being alive in the flesh. The dead may look after the afterwards. But the magnificent here and now of life in the flesh is ours, and ours alone and ours only for a time. We ought to dance with rapture that we should be alive and, in the flesh, and part of the living incarnate cosmos.

D. H. Lawrence

1

Curtain up

A new link on an infinite chain, Margerie entered the world in 1914. Born in Jamestown, New York, she was positioned in a place small enough to have a sense of community but large enough to be interesting. Blessed with loving parents, her life began harmoniously.

Encouraged to pursue her interests and be kind to others, it wasn't long before Margerie questioned why things happened or why they didn't. She was sociable, had a good sense of humor, and found everybody interesting. Even so, games that delighted playmates didn't stimulate her at all.

Drawn to the unconventional, she sensed she didn't belong on a traditional path. Her vaudevillian grandfather was a comfortable outsider who told her, "Whatever you do is performance for someone. Be happy, follow your dreams, and don't complain."

It was Margerie's turn. She sparkled in triumph, withdrew in tribulation, and after distressing events bounced back. Like everyone else, her time on earth was filled with unexpected surprises. Adventurous and independent, she dove into unfamiliar territory and if things got tough, played the cards that were dealt. Joy, despair, love and loss, are parts of a story worth telling. Margerie's journey was unusual but relatable; life is a paradox.

2

Providence

It was Margerie's favorite story. Over and over she asked her father how it happened, how he met Marie. He'd say he boarded a train for Manhattan on a winter morning, found a seat, then dozed off. After a nap Richard got up and headed for the dining car. As the train swerved, he jostled from to side and wondered what would be on the railroad menu; it was a lot more than lunch.

Seated with three jolly travelers headed home, he introduced himself and a conversation began. Max Lowenstein said he met Molly O'Brien on Manhattan's lower east side. When they were twelve, they sang on the street for change; six years later they got married. Marie was born a year after that. Doing a vaudeville act called "Max and Molly" they waited until their daughter could travel then performed across America. Nineteen, Marie was so dazzling Richard barely managed to steal a glance across the table. But as the train chugged through the Hudson River Valley, he loosened up and destiny intervened.

He told them about his hometown, how he loved music, finished college, and worked at the Jamestown Bank. Finishing a piece of apple pie, he finally looked directly at Marie. "It was the most peculiar thing," her father would say, "our eyes locked and something magical happened." Then came the part Margerie waited for. "Everything stopped, it really did. I froze up! There I was fork in the air, falling in love with your mother."

Marie and Richard got married that spring. They bought a two-story house with a big yard in Jamestown. Margerie joined them nine months later.

3

In your blood

Her mother played piano and as soon as Margerie could walk, she danced. She was four when her father left to fight in WW1; during his absence Marie had a baby boy. To honor Grandfather Max and husband Richard, Marie took front letters from both names and called him Maric. Good times returned after the war.

Independent, curious, and fun to be with, Margerie did well in school and liked who she was. When a substitute teacher called her Marge during roll call she didn't answer. Asked why she said, "It's not my name."

Every summer Max and Molly came to visit and brought souvenirs from places they'd performed. After begging them to do their vaudeville act, Margerie alerted the neighbors and filled the house with laughter and applause. But time passed and interests changed. Even though she was well liked and vice-president of her senior class, she didn't have much in common with fellow classmates. Her best friend, Helen Thorpe, came from Jamestown's richest family and she spent lots of time at Helen's impressive house. Fine art, meals prepared by a Portuguese chef, and stimulating conversations, opened a door to a waiting world.

In 1932 Marie surprised her daughter with a high-school graduation gift; a trip to Buffalo to see modern dance pioneer Lillian St. Mark. Paging through the program Margerie noticed company tryouts were the following day. On a whim, but with her mother's consent, she decided to audition.

They spent another night in a hotel waiting for the results. Unable to sleep she asked her mother a question. "Tell me the truth mom and be honest. Could it really happen? Those girls had more experience than I do."

"Of course it can happen, performing's in your blood." Turning on her side Marie ended the discussion. "Think positive and get some sleep!"

The next morning results were posted on the theater bulletin board; Margerie won the audition. Stunned but triumphant, she accepted the offer to join Llllian St. Mark's touring company.

A week later the girl from Jamestown boarded a train to join the troupe in Detroit. Waving goodbye from a seat by the window, she secretly wondered what she was doing. Eighteen and on her own Margerie smiled and plunged into the unknown.

4

Fluttering

Lillian St. Mark, tour manager Miss Edna, and four other girls were now family. As her mother predicted, St. Mark was a demanding prima donna who insisted on being called Madam. Flaming red hair and big crimson lips offset a pallid face; all that saved her from looking like a clown were bewitching green eyes. Entering a room with theatrical strides Madam's smile seemed welcoming until a commanding voice signaled she was in charge.

Steamer trunks filled with diaphanous fabrics were as important as the troupe. Madam designed the costumes then taught her girls how to twirl, twist, and undulate. During Margerie's first month St. Mark surprised her with a compliment. "Even though you're short, you're the best of the butterflies. Fluttering is an instinct. You either have it or you don't." That said she clapped her hands and said carry on.

Two things the boss wouldn't tolerate were drab and flab. Rife with rants, her rehearsals didn't end until every step was perfect. At first Margerie thought St. Mark's tirades were comical. When they became annoying, she joined the other girls and referred to Madam as "Shrill Lil."

What mattered most to the self-centered diva was performing without distraction. Refusing to deal with personal upsets, she told complainers to take their problems to Miss Edna. Staying afloat during countless squalls was a formidable task. Instead of a life jacket, Miss Edna kept a quart of gin stashed in her suitcase.

5

Name games

She'd never met anyone like Marianna Gariopa. Lillian St. Mark changed her "trash name" to Ellen Drake because it sounded refined. Even so her unruly nature continued. Claiming Margerie as an ally the day they met, Marianna had an idea. "Let's be echo sisters and call each other Mar. It'll drive Shrill Lil bananas!"

It wasn't long before Naughty Mar revealed a sordid past to the Mar from Jamestown. Her mother fled Portugal when she was fifteen and six months later gave birth to Marianna in the Bronx. "Uncles" came and went. If she asked her mother who her father was she'd venture he was Italian, Jewish, or from India; wasn't sure and didn't care. On her eleventh birthday Marianna got dumped in Pittsburgh with Aunt Babs, a spent but good-natured hooker who was no relation. For a few years they got postcards from Mexico but they stopped; no one knew if her mother was dead or alive. Shocked and concerned, Margerie tried being comforting but her friend had moved on. "Mar, you sweet thing. It wasn't so bad… Aunt Babs and I had lots of laughs. She taught me to dance, wear makeup, and all I needed to know about men."

Twenty, alluring, and clever, Ellen Drake was a perfect front for Marianna Gariopa. Her sophisticated guise coupled with a playful disposition rendered men helpless. When it came to hustling, she had a Ph.D. After a jealous dancer told Miss Edna that Ellen's jewelry was payment for making whoopee, the tour manager said, "Oh ya, so what. A girl's gotta grab what she can."

Wherever they landed Marianna found a suitor; corrupt or cultured they all were pushovers. In New Orleans a married man gave her diamond earrings. A week later an attorney in Atlanta bought her a gold bracelet and alligator handbag.

When they got to Cleveland, she met a circuit court judge. Two dates later pretending to need dental surgery, she sobbed hysterically and left Ohio with $900. At first Margerie was shocked by Ellen Drake's behavior, secretly she found it thrilling.

The troupe spent four months a year in Boston where St. Mark based her company. On a blustery day during lunch in Cambridge the two Mars considered their future. "I've been hoofing with that old cunt for four years," Marianna grumbled, then poked at her Dover sole. Enough is enough. I've got $4,000 at Allied Federal and it's time to spread my wings. You'll see Mar, I'm gonna fly right."

Margerie wasn't sure what she meant but glancing at the weather outside agreed they should be someplace else. Tired of Shrill Lil and gypsy living it was time for a change. "The hell with this," naughty Mar said. "We should be where the sun shines and the money is. Why wait? It's time to shake things up. Girls like us belong in Hollywood."

6

1937

Performing in nineteen states Margerie met mayors, maestros, and socialites. She swam in the Atlantic and Pacific Oceans, saw the Grand Canyon, Mississippi River, and Blue Ridge Mountains. But after three years nomadic life grew tiresome. An abrasive egomaniac, St. Mark's tyrannical rants became unbearable.

Ellen Drake quit without notice and took off for Los Angeles. It wasn't long before she met Texas cattle baron, Hank Seebar, at a party in Beverly Hills. Sixty, beefy, and filthy rich, he was looking for a trophy wife. Marianna would settle for luxury and freedom. After getting married in Dallas, they moved into a twenty-room house with a maid, cook, chauffeur, and forty-foot swimming pool.

Four months later Margerie finally left Madam, Miss Edna, and four dancing dunces, to set out on her own. Eager to act and reorganize her life, she packed her bags and took hope to Hollywood.

7

Another Drake

Marianna said Daniel Drake knew all she needed to know about the movie game. After settling into a Hollywood boarding house Margerie dropped a nickel in a pay phone and called. Upbeat and friendly, Daniel said Ellen Drake told him all about "the other Mar" and suggested they meet for lunch the following day.

She found the restaurant and knew at once the stunning young man waiting by the door was him. "Daniel?" she said. Stepping forward he grinned then gave her a hug. "Don't tell me, I know who you are! Should I call you Marigold, Martha, or Mar? Marianna had so many selves I couldn't keep track." Laughing together, they formed a bond.

Margerie couldn't help staring; Daniel was gorgeous. Slender with wavy black hair and dark brown eyes, his sensual smile was oddly suggestive. He told her after dropping out of college he left

Philadelphia, then told her why. "Boring place Philly… one long nap. I'm really a dago named Gino Varconi, got dry-cleaned here into Daniel Drake. Marianna and I pretended to be brother and sister - Danny and Ellen Drake. What a roar, two phony aristocrats!" He took a sip of mint tea. "Believe you me hon, I party hard but keeping up with her was exhausting."

Three hours flew by. Daniel had a featured part in a western that was premiering in three weeks and asked her to come. "You'll be my date so dress to the nines Dollface. Everything here is about looking the part. It's fun but exhausting." He ordered more tea then lit a cigarette. "There's a party afterwards at the Roosevelt so you'll meet some people and we'll drink ourselves silly. But be prepared, I'm gonna push you right into the swamp."

Gino Varconi was a lot like Marianna Gariopa, and Daniel was a lot like Ellen Drake. She wrote her friend about their meeting, the upcoming premiere, where she'd moved, and gave her the number of the phone in the hall. When Mar called, she emphasized how much she liked Danny.

"You mean my brother?" she laughed. "Honey, he's a class act. An absolute riot. Of all the nancies he's the best!"

Margery sounded puzzled. "The what?"

"Oh Mar, you've got to be kidding? Can't you tell? Now listen to mama. In this town queers are the best friends to have. The girls want you dead, the men want you naked. Danny drinks too much but he'll watch your back."

A bit disappointed she decided Marianna was right; a buddy was better than a boyfriend. A week later she got a package from Mar, now Mrs. Ellen Seebar. Inside was a strand of pearls and two pendant earrings, things she'd scored years ago from an attorney in St. Louis. Marianna called it 'prenuptial stuff' and said to wear it at the premiere.

On opening night klieg lights sent beams of light into the California sky. Fans shouted and photographers scrambled for position as they walked a red carpet into the theater. Danny had a good part, played a handsome roughrider. When he died with an arrow in his back, every female sighed.

By the time they got to the hotel ballroom a twelve-piece orchestra was in full swing. Scanning the glamorous crowd, she saw Myrna Loy, Clark Gable, and familiar faces from the silver screen. Already on his second martini, Danny was unimpressed. "Well here we are watching the dragons dance." Then noticing someone approaching their table, groaned, "Oh God, here she comes. Rhonda Twit."

A portly bald man with a camera moved towards them. "Hey cowboy, nice job in that saddle!" Grinning he introduced himself to the young lady. "Ron Dewitt, studio photographer. And aren't you a pretty thing! What's your name sweetheart."

Lighting up she smiled. "Thank you, Mr. Dewitt. I'm new in town. My name's Margerie, Margerie Summers."

"Delighted to meet you newbie. Let's get a shot. C'mon now, you two snuggle up." A flashbulb went off and he had his picture. "Trust me dear, you're in safe hands." Leering at Danny he winked and was on his way. "Toodles, gotta go now. Lots of egos to massage."

Danny picked at a fruit plate. "And that, dear viewer, is the cartoon this evening. Beneath that blubber lurks a rattlesnake, one of many you'll find slithering through the tumbleweeds." Reaching for her hand he said, "C'mon girl, let's show these baboons how to dance."

And dance they did. Sweeping across the floor Daniel introduced her around. "Better watch this girl" he'd say or "Take a good look: Star quality!" Overwhelmed and dazzled, Margerie ended up in three photos. One was with James Cagney.

It was after two when Daniel dropped her off. Suggesting he get a good night's sleep she watched his lips curl provocatively. "I don't think so Mars bar. My night's just starting." Looking mischievous he said goodbye then drove off into the night. She had to wonder. Where was he was going?

8

Wasn't sure

Making it in Hollywood wasn't as easy as twirling around a ballroom with Daniel Drake. Focused and determined, Margerie took elocution lessons, found an agent, auditioned, and worked as an extra to stay afloat. When a stylist told her the golden look was out, she became a redhead and got new head shots. When the trend changed a casting director suggested she go back to being a blonde. After testing at MGM her agent said she'd nailed it. But she didn't; the producer's girlfriend did.

A shot at stardom in sunny California required tolerance for hot air, vicious rivalry, and unscrupulous politics. When a casting director asked her how she felt about "giving head" she had no idea what he was talking about so said she "wasn't sure." Asking Daniel what he meant, he told her after he stopped laughing. She thought he was joking.

Refusing to "do anything" for a break, Margerie

realized Hollywood wasn't just about talent; she was competing in a whorehouse. Every week a fresh flock of young women arrived ready to do whatever was necessary to get ahead. Even extra work got hard to find. Refusing to give up she took a temporary job in a department store to stay afloat. A year later she was still selling hosiery.

On a warm winter morning her father called with horrible news. Headed for the Palace Theater, grandparents Max and Molly died on a bus that crashed outside of Wilkes-Barre. Heavily sedated, her mother had been put in bed.

All Margerie cared about fit into a single suitcase. There was nothing to tie up or anyone she'd miss except Daniel and a Bavarian woman who lived next door. Two days later she boarded an eastbound train with three oranges, two sandwiches, and a candy bar. The sun was shining like it always did as the train pulled out of the station. Gazing out the window she'd seen enough; reached over and pulled down the shade.

HOME AGAIN

9

Little Star

She'd been on screen for less than a minute in *Ships Ahoy*, said "Good morning" in *City Girl*, and appeared in a classroom scene behind Judy Garland. Beyond that she'd been part of a crowd; an extra. But in Jamestown it didn't matter. Their hometown girl was somebody special.

The Chronicle did a full page spread on Margerie Summers with a photo of Lillian St. Mark, a Hollywood headshot, and a picture of her vaudevillian grandparents.

The following week the mayor's wife dropped by with an angel food cake and a proposal. Due to the recession, the City Center had an empty rehearsal hall they'd gladly donate if she'd open a dance and dramatics studio.

It was a good opportunity. Marie could play piano, Margerie would teach, and she'd make a living. To the delight of young hopefuls and doting mothers, *Little Star Studio* opened for business a month later.

10

Crazy or what

Life in Hollywood was challenging; there were days when buying a donut seemed extravagant. But now the slender, stylish blonde had come home. Perceived as someone with worldly experience, her sophisticated profile gave *Little Star* a promising start.

Tony Regato, her brother's best friend, was a freshman when she was a high school senior. During a break from touring with Lillian St. Mark, he came into the parlor to say hello. Seventeen and strikingly handsome, after he left with Maric to shoot hoops her mother said, "Now there's a guy who belongs in the movies."

After college Tony returned to Jamestown to help his father expand Regato Construction. Like Margerie, his youthful achievements and good looks stood out in a town beaten down by a bad economy. In a way they both were outsiders. Five years since they'd seen each other, Tony dropped by to sign his sister up for a class at *Little Star*. Bending down he encouraged the shy eight-year-old to say hello. His gentle manner caught Margerie off guard. When he looked up their eyes locked and something happened. It felt like an adrenaline rush. Both of them felt awkward and surprised. Tony gave her a check then politely left with his sister.

It didn't make sense. Tony was Maric's friend, a kid from the neighborhood she'd seen grow up. She replayed the incident over and over then told her mother. "It's like what happened to you and Dad on the train... one look then everything stopped." Margerie stood up, took a few steps, then turned and sat back down. "Like a dunce I said see you around. Are you kidding? When he left I felt like half of me went with him. He's all I think about. Tony Regato, my brother's buddy… am I crazy or what?"

11

Cradle snatch

Tony was twenty-two, Margerie was twenty-six. In 1939 their romance raised a few eyebrows. Helen Thorpe teased her for robbing the cradle and left it at that. But single women hoping to reel in the hottest catch in Jamestown took it more seriously. And so did their mothers. As far as they were concerned, a theatrical vamp had seduced their most eligible bachelor.

Both families were supportive and if they hadn't been it wouldn't have mattered. Focusing on their projects, Margerie taught seven classes a week while Tony supervised construction of a wing at Municipal Hospital. On Sundays they spent time with their families then snuck off to a cabin on Chautauqua Lake. To no one's surprise Tony proposed a year later and gave his temptress a diamond ring.

12

Who cares?

Pleased with the response to *Little Star*, Margerie gazed out the window and watched Jamestown's only pink Cadillac pull up in front of the studio. Florene Cieplak, a buxom redhead from "pigeon alley," was behind the wheel. After seducing the heir to Jamestown's biggest factory and a shotgun wedding, she delivered twin boys. Daisy popped out a year later.

From an impressive house on Burberry Road, a determined mother made sure her daughter got everything she'd been denied. Fifteen, sassy, and spoiled, Daisy wore expensive clothes, gold jewelry, had big breasts like her mother, and loved being stared it.

They came in, sat down, and Florene started jabbering. "I'm so excited, this is going to be huge. A fortune teller told me Daisy would be a star and to look for signs. Inevitable, that's what she said! When *Little Star* opened I knew it was an omen."

Looking at her daughter she continued gushing. "This gypsy was the real thing. I could tell. She showed me the tea leaves and there it was, inside the cup!"

Sullenly chewing gum, tomorrow's movie star glanced at her lacquered nails, frowned and acted like she wanted to go. Familiar with deluded mothers Margerie let Florene deflate then took her check.

Every Wednesday Daisy sauntered in with Selena Pratt, another offspring of rich but clueless parents. Smelling like clove gum and cigarettes they giggled then indifferently did their routines. One afternoon they were loitering by their teacher's desk when Tony dropped by. Reluctantly, she introduced them to her handsome fiancé. Selena was speechless but Daisy thrust out her chest, extended a hand, and grinned at him salaciously.

After he left Selena came out of her trance. "Gee Miss Summers, he's really good looking! When you getting married?" Pretending to be busy Margerie shuffled papers and said she wasn't sure.

Whispering wildly they turned to leave, but on the way out Daisy's take on Tony was loud and clear. "Really Selena" she said as the door was closing, "you're such a prude. Who cares if they're engaged? I'd fuck him."

13

Thanksgiving

Looking forward to a summer wedding, both families joined together for Thanksgiving. Guests from 4 to 87 climbed the steps of the Regatos' house to celebrate. Children raced after Tony's dog, men smoked cigars on the front porch, and pies baked in the oven. Wives and mothers prepared the feast then put platters of turkey, pasta, breads, and salads on tables set with bottles of Tuscan wine. Toasts were made, stories told, and joy filled every room.

Before leaving Mrs. Regato handed Margerie a lace veil she wore at her own wedding. "It carries love from a happy marriage," she said. "May you and Tony have the same good fortune!"

Agreeing on a Catholic marriage they reserved June 6th at St. Joseph's. Margerie wanted Helen Thorpe as maid of honor and Marianna for a bridesmaid. Tony chose Maric to be his best man. The reception would be in a hall facing Chatauqua Lake and the Regatos were planning the menu. Paging through magazines the bride-to-be searched for the perfect wedding dress.

Even though she began each morning with a prayer of thanks, she worried. Horrors ravaged Europe, the economy teetered, and instability surrounded the globe. Even though *Little Star* gave scholarships to the needy and she volunteered at a nursing home on Monday nights, it didn't feel like enough. For two years everything fell into place; now she wondered if good fortune would continue.

Her mother told her to expect the unexpected, events are unpredictable; think positive and carry on. But alone in her room at night she feared reversals. And it didn't pass. Waves of anxiety passed through her for the first time.

14

Brooklyn brother

His cousin was the big brother Tony never had. Marco left Brooklyn every summer to spend two weeks in Jamestown. They fished together at Willow Creek, built a tree house together, and slept under tents made of sheets. When Tony got older they wandered the beach at Chautauqua Lake where Marco taught him about girls, how to get their attention and keep them talking.

Before joining the Navy, his cousin spent a weekend in Jamestown. Tony snuck a bottle of wine out of the house and under a full moon listened to Marco talk about a girl in Bensonhurst. "Vitalia moved to the neighborhood a year ago and was so gorgeous I couldn't deal with it. On Sundays I'd see her in church and made sure to say hello to her parents." Tony never saw him smoke before and watched Marco light a cigarette "On Easter I got my nerve up, asked her dad on the steps of St. Ann's if

I could take his daughter out." Together they watched a perfect smoke ring float towards the moon. "You know those old school guys, this big Sicilian is staring bullets at me. Finally he says okay, you pick her up Saturday at 7 and get her home by 10:30. Then he warns me, says you're late, finito. I said deal and we shook hands."

Tony hoped Marco would talk about sex like they had last summer. "Did you make out? Was she like that crazy Puerto Rican girl you told me about?"

Marco grinned at his fifteen-year-old cousin. "Sorry cuz, it's not like that. We saw a movie, held hands, and that was it. It's all about respect. Remember I said this, she's the one." He took another swig of chianti then shared his plan. "After I get some rank in the Navy I'll marry that girl. And I'm telling her dad that before I leave. You'll see Tony, no more bullshit. I'm gonna lay it all out... I got my eyes on the prize."

15

Red Pontiac

Eighteen days before Christmas, Margerie and her fiancé strolled downtown. They walked around the manger set up in the Village Square, stopped for hot chocolate, then looked at decorations in the store windows. Passing a lot stacked with fir trees, pungent pine filled the cold air. As tiny snowflakes drifted down Tony felt a surge of joy, pulled the woman he loved in close and stole a kiss.

They couldn't miss Dan Porter's bright red Pontiac barreling down Center Street. When he pulled over they thought he was going to offer them a ride. Instead, he looked troubled, rolled down a window and shattered winter bliss. "Bad news you guys, it's all over the radio. The Japs bombed Pearl Harbor. It was a total massacre." Stunned, they got into his car and headed home.

Margerie settled in for a restless night. She thought about people she'd met in towns and cities across the country. She knew they were frightened, unprepared like she was. When the sun had risen in every state, the rich, poor, old, and young, huddled around radios waiting to hear President Roosevelt. He confirmed what everyone feared; America was at war.

16

Schedules and plans

What Marco hoped for actually happened; he became a naval lieutenant and married Vitalia. When his daughter was born he asked Tony to be her godfather.

On a sunny Hawaiian morning he was on deck drinking coffee with a group of sailors. Suddenly without warning, the Japanese flew over Pearl Harbor. The sneak attack killed 417 men on his ship. Two sailors survived but Marco wasn't one of them. Thousands of Americans were slaughtered in half an hour.

Mrs. Regato left for Brooklyn to comfort her sister while the rest of the family grieved. Tony insisted on being left alone; there was nothing to talk about. Predictably, sorrow evolved into outrage. Two days later he got up before anyone else, ate breakfast, and walked into town. By noon he'd enlisted in the army.

Everything changed, schedules and plans collapsed. Margerie pleaded with Tony to get married right away but he refused, said they should wait until after the war, when things got better. But it wasn't his reason; he wouldn't let the woman he adored be trapped in marriage if he returned disabled.

At the end of January her fiancé boarded a bus with fourteen men headed for boot camp. Families and friends cheered them on. Wearing a red scarf and matching mittens Margerie stood shivering in the snow. When Tony saw her she raised an arm and waved robotically. Trying to smile she bit into her lip, then tasting blood watched the man she loved leave Jamestown.

17

On a mission

In six weeks, he'd be done with boot camp. Margerie sent him letters scented with cologne, imagined laughing again at a family table or strolling along Chautauqua Lake. But all he could give was twenty-eight hours before shipping out of Manhattan.

After her train pulled into Grand Central, Tony was waiting. Outside soldiers and sailors roamed the streets in swarms. They looked strong, confident, eager to get on with things. Who, she wondered, could stop these brave young princes of America?

Their room in an old hotel had a hissing radiator and window facing the alley but it didn't matter. They got into bed, attached themselves, and by eight o'clock Tony was sleeping. Curled up against his warm body she listened to him breathe until dawn. They made love again and checked out at noon.

After buying hotdogs and soda from a vendor on the street, they sat on an empty bench in Times Square. Watching people pass by was distracting but Tony kept checking his watch. With orders to assemble on Pier 47 at 2:30, he took her arm and they walked to the west side.

Alone, or with their people, every kind of soldier gathered on the crowded dock. Proud but worried parents embraced boys becoming men too soon. Youthful dreams had vanished; their sons were on a mission to save the world.

An appropriate background, shrill whistles and garbled announcements interrupted a monotone of blurry voices. Letting go was awkward, unrehearsed, embraces abruptly ended. Margerie could tell Tony was about to disengage. He held her and whispered, "I love you," then braced himself, turned, and took off. She watched him move towards the mammoth carriers then disappear into a khaki sea. Tony's girl leaned against a wire fence and feeling faint slumped to the ground. She cried until no tears were left.

18

Halloween

It was the day before Halloween, ten months since Tony left. She asked his sister Rosalie to join her for a walk downtown. They looked at carved pumpkins lining the town square, got ice cream cones, a comic book, picked up trick-or-treat candy, then started home.

A perfect autumn day, she felt grateful for being in Jamestown. It was crisp and sunny. Beneath the deep blue sky, red and yellow leaves carpeted big front lawns. A neighbor drove by, honked and waved, then turning the corner Tony's dog raced to greet them.

Margerie could see the Regatos' house through a haze of burning leaves but for some reason it looked different, seemed dark and uninviting. When they reached the front yard, something felt wrong; the air seemed thin, she felt muscles tighten. Waves of anxiety rushed through her then she heard a voice from inside the house. Tony's father was crying out, "Oh God…my boy!" Her heart started pounding, she could hardly breathe then stumbled. Rosalie laughed, twirled on the grass like they were playing a game. But something cruel had gathered force, Margerie was closing down. The only mercy was fainting onto a pile of leaves someone had raked in Tony's yard.

19

Not anywhere

A year ago, before Thanksgiving, they were in St. Joseph's planning their wedding with a priest. Now they were together again: Margerie in the front pew, Tony in a casket twelve feet away, and Father Basile saying a funeral mass. Her mother held her hand, Mrs. Regato was weeping. Tony's college friends, relatives from Brooklyn, shopkeepers, construction workers, and people she'd didn't know, filled the church. Grim, rumbling chords poured from a cathedral organ and someone sang. Then it was silent; two men in black suits appeared and wheeled her fiancé away.

Margerie held onto her father as she left and tried not to look at anyone. But towards the back of the church she saw an old man sitting alone and crying. Mr. Grunwald lived two doors away from the Regato's house. After losing his wife he turned sour, became the neighborhood grouch everyone avoided. Then something happened. Tony was eleven that winter, unasked and unpaid he shoveled the grumpy man's walk. Then he did it every year. If he walked by and there was a paper on the lawn he picked it up and laid it by his door. If he was riding his bike and saw him on the porch he waved. By the time he started high school Tony called him Earl, dropped by every week to see if he needed anything. His friends teased him; nobody liked Mr. Grunwald. But Tony did.

His loss accelerated her grief. Margerie leaned against her father and buried her face. Nobody, not anyone, could quell the pain. She prayed to be taken but there was no place to go. No opening, nothing. Not anywhere.

20

Maric

When he was a boy Maric loved running, swinging on ropes, and climbing trees. Well mannered, he did whatever his parents asked. A good brother, good son, and nice guy, he became a popular high-school athlete.

His best friend since fourth grade, Maric and Tony swam and skated on Chautauqua Lake, played tennis, football, and shot endless hoops together. Senior year they took a forty-mile hike along the Colorado River. Even though he teased him, he wasn't surprised when Tony fell in love with his sister. It made sense; he was family.

After Marco died he watched his friend suffer. When Tony enlisted, he did too. Now an honor guard at his funeral, Maric shouldered grief and stood strong. That night he held Margery until she cried herself to sleep. When everyone was in bed he took off. Two days later he returned looking haggard and drained. Respecting his "private side," no one asked where he'd been. The next morning before anybody got up, he left a note on the kitchen table saying he'd been called back to his base in California.

On a plane in a seat by the window, he watched clouds go by then replaced by random new forms. Sealing himself off felt protective and nurtured his anger. His need for retribution solidified, it was a gesture of love. When Maric landed a galvanized warrior emerged; hungry for recompense, ready for war.

21

Mothers

Raised by a Catholic mother and Jewish father, Marie's parents were empathetic vaudevillians. Her unorthodox childhood fostered a cheerful nature and flexible take on things. It was a quality she shared with her husband and children.

Marie's unstructured belief was God is love. If things got tough she encouraged whoever needed it to have faith. Sunday services weren't mandatory but on Christmas Eve the family attended midnight mass. Occasionally Margerie visited an Episcopal church with Helen Thorpe. Family policy was lenient; and enlightenment was a personal journey.

Margerie's mother was supportive and kept her busy after Tony died. A year later Marie's disposition abruptly changed. Distant and preoccupied, even her comforting smile looked forced. When her husband put a hand on her breast it felt hard as a rock; the next day he took her to the hospital. After a series of tests, the doctor said it was cancer so advanced there wasn't much anyone could do.

Marie called June "the happy month" because it was bursting with life. After leaving home to be treated for pain, she only saw summer from a hospital window. Every day after teaching class Margerie walked to Municipal Medical to sit with her. One afternoon Marie had something to share. "For three days I heard her calling. She was saying my name but I couldn't see her. Last night mother came again, stood right where you are. She said they were waiting and not to be afraid." Sure she'd see Max and Molly again, Marie seemed peaceful and drifted off.

The next morning her father woke Margerie up. Marie had passed on. Minutes later Maric walked into her room, the family dog beside him. Sunlight streaming through a window felt inappropriate. She wanted to get up, close the blinds, but didn't. The three of them sat on the bed. When their father started sobbing, his son put an arm on his shoulders and Margerie took his hand. The dog looked up, made a sad noise, and they wept together.

22

Perseverance

Another wound refused to heal. Margerie avoided making plans and had no opinions. When her father asked if he should paint the house, she said she wasn't sure. If they were dining out she didn't know what to order; would get what someone else was having.

Cutting back, she taught two classes at *Little Star*. The rest of the week an Italian couple gave ballroom dancing lessons.

Margerie found someone to clean the house and do laundry but dutifully cooked for her father. Anxious to retire due to arthritis, Richard Summers considered moving to California where Maric lived. When he asked his daughter what she thought she couldn't answer because she didn't know. Feeling abandoned and depressed, Margerie did what people expected: she persevered.

NEW YORK CITY
THE 1950S

23

Mar and Ellen Seebar

The Mar in Dallas, now Ellen Seebar, never gave up on her best friend. Year after year she asked the Mar in Jamestown to meet her in Manhattan. "I've got that green so help me spend it!" When she tried again in 1949, Margerie finally said yes.

The only time she'd been in New York City was with Tony. She remembered making love in a rundown hotel, holding hands while walking to the docks, and a final kiss before he left. But she'd forgotten the city's hypnotic pull. The moment she got off the train Manhattan's legendary vitality took control.

Joining the crowded street, she walked to the curb and hailed a cab. Exhaust fumes merged with a profusion of city noise bouncing through a rolled down window. The noxious smell was replaced by chestnuts roasting on a cart, then yielded to the stench of her cabbie's cigar. Horns honked and traffic stalled as awe and chaos seduced her. Unable to focus on a single aspect, she eagerly joined the circus.

Five years since they'd seen each other, the sophisticated Ellen Seebar opened the door to a plush two-bedroom suite in the Plaza Hotel. A blue satin dress with a tight cinched waist showed off a figure men drooled over. Glossy black hair, now stylish and bouffant, made her look like movie star Ava Gardner.

"At last, my soulmate. I don't need to perform for those Texas goons! And it's about time Mar, we both deserve a break." Then off she went. "Dallas is one crazy ride. It's rich, wild, and wicked, but honey it wears me out. You should hear 'em… all that talk about cattle, oil, and football. And those phony blondes are backstabbing airheads!"

Ellen Seebar lit a cigarette, drank another glass of champagne, then reverted to being Marianna Gariopa. "I'll tell you this, those bimbos see me and they head for the hills. And they should Mar" she admitted, "those Texas boys are ready to saddle up. And I'm queen of the Dallas rodeo." Slapping a hip she squealed, "Woo-hah, giddy up!" Margerie laughed, took a gulp of bubbly, and felt like she was coming out of a coma.

Thrilled to be with her only real friend, Marianna laid out the plans. "Now listen up. Tonight we'll have dinner downstairs then I've got tickets for *Kiss Me Kate*. Tomorrow we shop 'til we drop and it's all on Hank." When Margerie objected, she got shut down. "Don't go silly on me Mar, those are the rules. Daddy's no joyride. Most of the time he's gone or getting hammered with his posse. His crowd calls it 'the Dallas double'... barbecue and bourbon. And besides, Hank Seebar is filthy rich. When I'm not spending he worries, thinks shopping keeps me busy. And honey what he doesn't know," she winked, "keeps me from going crazy."

For two days spend they did. Wherever they went heads turned; visually and verbally Ellen Seebar demanded attention. They got dresses from Saks, shoes at Bonwit's, and bought more at Bergdorf's. The day after that they hit Madison Avenue for lingerie and sweaters. Over the top, indulgence was just what a depleted woman needed.

After Margerie learned Hank Seebar had 200,000 acres that kept him out of Dallas for weeks at a time, Marianna told her about a rendezvous with the son of a tycoon who lived next door. At a party celebrating his graduation from Princeton, the good-looking twenty-three-year-old was hot to trot with Ellen Seebar so they snuck off and had stand-up sex in the garage. Looking pleased with herself she said the affair went on for months. Seeing the frown on her friend's face she justified the fling. "Now Mar, don't you be judging me. It was a neighborly thing. I was welcoming him home."

Assuming cattlemen considered their wives to be personal property, Marianna's reckless lifestyle was troubling. In spite of being Ellen Seebar she'd do what she wanted. Finishing a second bottle of wine they talked about things they shared with no one else. Bemoaning her life in Jamestown, Margerie admitted after losing Tony, then her mother, she too had passed on. Marianna lit another cigarette and zeroed in.

"Now hear this Mar, you gotta get out of there. It's time to move on. You've been living with dead people. You can do that later!"

"Easy to say, where would I go?" Margerie paused. "And what would I do?"

"Where? Knock-knock. What the hell are you talking about?" Naughty Mar had the answer. "Right here. Take a good look, you know I'm right. Theater, art, interesting people… and lots of men if you haven't noticed. You could do all sorts of things in New York. Look at what you've done, a dancer, actress, teacher. Do you want to stay in Hicksville? You belong here, I can feel it."

"It's not that easy. I'm thirty-four."

Marianna shot back. "Come on Mar, give me a break. Thirty-four, forty-four, so what. Maybe you should dig a grave. Sounds like you're ready to bury."

Changing the subject, she laid out plans for the following day. "Tomorrow I got us appointments at Arden's: a nine-to-five overhaul. They'll do hair, nails, makeup, and we'll get a massage. When they're through with you it'll break a mirror. You've let yourself go Mar, but that's over. Time to get back in the saddle." Ellen Seebar corrected herself. "Wait a minute, did I just say that? I sound like a roughrider!" Laughing together they finished their drinks then went to bed.

Escalating her campaign Marianna made inquiries; the best hotel for women was the Barbizon on East Sixty-Third. After a day of beauty, they dropped by, the hotel, picked up brochures, and got an application. Genteel and sophisticated it was a perfect choice. Naughty Mar looked pleased. "So there you have it, no excuses. What are you waiting for? Time to move on."

Leaving home was easier than she thought. After telling her father, she tied things up. Six weeks later Margerie checked into the Barbizon. Turning a key she entered her room, stood by the window, and gazed at the city lights. Everything felt right; she belonged in Manhattan.

24

Gee

Like the Upper East Side neighborhood it stood in, the Barbizon was pricey. Heavy with graduates from schools like Vassar, Smith, and Sarah Lawrence, most of the young women in the residential hotel came from wealth. Working as secretaries, models, or in publishing, they shared the goal of marriage, money, and living as well or better than their parents. Polite but cliquish, she found them bland and boring. Hoping to act again, Margerie had to make a living so found a temporary job as a receptionist.

She met Liddy Becker when she knocked on her door and asked to borrow a nail file. Pudgy, insecure, and graduate of a junior college, she came from a rich family but lacked the finesse of a Barbizon girl. After learning her neighbor was an actress, she invited Margerie to see *Death of a*

Salesman; then asked her parents to send two tickets a week for a Broadway show. Margerie saw the best of American theater from orchestra seats but had little in common with her lonely companion.

Seeing a Broadway production every weekend had its price. Liddy was uncomfortable talking about herself so asked lots of questions. When she discovered her older friend lived in Hollywood and knew Daniel Drake she gasped, "Really? You actually talked to him?" After learning Margerie's fiancé was killed in the war, she thought about it then said, "Gee, that must've made you sad."

After four months in the Barbizon, Margerie decided it, and the neighborhood, was too genteel. Searching for a more diverse environment, she began exploring the city.

25

The Village

Anxious to leave the rarified world of the Upper East Side, Margerie ventured downtown on a Sunday at the end of May. Climbing up from the subway to Sheridan Square, the mystique of Greenwich Village waited to embrace her.

Sixty blocks from The Barbizon, she discovered a different world. Nothing seemed uniform or contrived; the pace was different and she could see the sky. In contrast to the city's numerical grid, streets had names like Leroy, Carmine, Christopher, and Bleecker, that veered off in unpredictable directions. Dignified brownstones stood close to houses built in the 1800s; Georgian Revivals were a block away from Italianate townhouses. Around the corner a long stretch of brick-tenements held their ground and provided immigrants, blue collar workers, and unconventional occupants with low priced rentals. Bakeries, markets, bars, and restaurants popped up next to shops selling books, antiques, clothes, and jewelry. Historic, eccentric, and surprising, Greenwich Village was an enclave where nothing repeated itself.

New Yorkers let Greenwich stay in Connecticut and referred to this part of their city as "the Village." Permeated with tolerance it was a sanctuary for free spirits. Rich, poor, cultured or not, everyone seemed content. And no one was in much of a hurry.

At the edge of Washington Square old men competed with scholars and vagabonds moving knights and bishops over cement chessboards. Inside the park musicians played guitars, accordions, and violins behind open instrument cases waiting for donations. A woman smoking a cigar had a top hat on, was pushing a baby buggy with two chickens in it. A juggler with six oranges spinning in the air stood ten feet away from a husky baritone singing an aria from *Barber of Seville*. By the fountain, Margerie watched a magician in a purple cape do tricks; then held out a dollar so the monkey on his shoulder could grab it.

She stopped and listened to a long-haired young man read a poem about the girl he loved then lost. When he finished, she stood there; alone, overwhelmed, and grateful. She'd never seen anything like Washington Square.

Euphoria was exhausting, so she found an outdoor table at a cafe on Thompson Street and ordered an espresso. Years of embedded sorrow surrendered to interest and delight. In a place where everything seemed acceptable, Margerie felt tears of joy stream down her face. A daunting, unpredictable city had pried open her soul and now, regardless of what would come, she was alive again.

26

Elliot

Margerie belonged downtown. A week after answering a Roommate Wanted ad in *The Villager*, she moved into a fourth-floor walk-up on MacDougal Street. Sharing space with costume designer Roz Guttman was a good fit. A savvy native born in Queens, Roz approached work the way she handled her love life: pragmatically. Her new roommate was not as sensible.

Men who survived a gruesome war came home. Artists, musicians, and writers flocked to Greenwich Village where they met liberated women in bars, cafes, and parties that went on until dawn. Margerie found these renegades appealing and got involved with a self-centered painter who lived off a small inheritance. Elliot drank more than he painted and if he disagreed with what someone said, would condescendingly say "Get real." Certain that love would heal existential wounds she ignored his flaws.

Not very nice, he'd done it twice. After he cancelled a date for the third time, she decided to go to a party with Roz. In the corner of a crowded room she saw her lover locked in a kiss while squeezing the breast of a wild-looking redhead. Disengaging, he spotted her and glared; then got back to business. Margerie rushed home in tears.

He didn't see her, but she got a glimpse of Elliot walking his dog the following week. A month later through a window on the bus, Margerie saw him crossing the street with a young Asian woman. They were laughing. That was the last time she saw him.

27

Cuspidor

Nursing a broken heart, she ventured out on her own. Alone in a bar or café she met men effortlessly and if she felt like it, jumped into bed. Beyond that, she couldn't be bothered; second dates were of no interest. Appalled when Margerie claimed it was liberation instead of promiscuity, Roz convinced her to seek professional help.

A retired therapist who had heard it all, Dr. Shenk donated time at Chelsea Clinic to help those with limited incomes. He encouraged Margerie to examine her lifestyle, focus on goals, and discover what generated impulsive choices. When they talked about sex, he explained some men would say anything to fulfill desire; then he got to the point. "Women who casually yield tarnish the vessel. Using the body only for pleasure, they become seminal spittoons."

She'd seen them in movies, dented brass cuspidors on grimy barroom floors. Accommodating but vile, they held the refuse of distasteful men. The sordid image stayed in her mind.

Two months later Margerie started a class at The Actors Studio, had a job at Village Books, and avoided temptation by baby-sitting on Saturday nights. Roz was impressed. Therapy worked wonders.

Anxious to share her breakthrough with women who had lost their way, Margerie urged whoever would listen to be prudent. "Men will do anything to get you in bed," she'd tell them, "then off they'll go on their merry way." To be more explicit, she'd paint a picture. "He'll be out the door when he's through with you. And there you'll be, alone on the bed. Used and dirty... holding his waste like a seminal spittoon."

28

Yes I can

If someone asked where she was raised, she'd say in a wonderful place. And that was true. But Jamestown was a town with traditions that required moderation. Churches encouraged their flocks to stay within boundaries and endure their burdens; a spiritual culture Margerie found restrictive. Interested in the before-and-after as much as the present, she was drawn to the inexplicable. New York City was a perfect setting.

Acting and income were undependable, but she was in a city filled with books on metaphysics, mysticism, and different faiths. Study and meditation helped her endure misfortune, but a series of disappointments wore her down.

Despite persistence, auditions proved fruitless. Thirty-eight, Margerie was too old, too short, and unknown; no one seemed interested. Even though she worked five days a week at Village Books and taught elocution to several aspiring actors, she could barely afford lessons at Actor's Studio. There were days she simply stayed in bed.

When a friend invited her to a Hilliard Parker lecture, "Yes You Can," she had nothing to lose but a Sunday morning. Sitting in Town Hall she listened to what the metaphysical teacher said. Combining mental discipline with spiritual law was so inspiring she bought one of his books to read that night.

The next morning she looked into a mirror and repeated Dr. Parker's advice: "Yes I Can!" A dozen women were trying out at The Actor's Studio for the role of Blanche Dubois in *Streetcar Named Desire*. After a shower she put on makeup, got dressed, grabbed the script and started walking. Block after block she repeated the affirmation over and over. When the studio was in sight, she said it out loud then said it again. "Yes I Can!" Shoulders back and standing straight, Margerie walked in, took a seat, and waited to audition.

29

A run in Heaven

The office manager at The Actor's Studio was a friend and called first. She'd overheard Collie Berg say he was casting Margerie as Blanche Dubois, the coveted part in *Streetcar Named Desire*.

For years she had questioned her talent; finally, an opportunity to excel presented itself. Rehearsals began in July and continued for two exhausting months. Week after week she let raw emotion surface, then dragged herself home, ate supper, and fell into bed.

A character of eerie familiarity, Blanche Dubois became Margerie's obsession. Collie's direction touched every nerve. Her fragile portrayal was so haunting other players seemed peripheral, but the play evolved into a remarkable ensemble production.

After outstanding reviews, the autumn showcase quickly sold out. The Village Voice wrote, "Miss Summers is hypnotic, you can't stop watching her. Her Blanche is vulnerable, affecting, like a chloroformed butterfly fluttering inside a glass jar." The Times described her performance as "illumined, ethereally nuanced... she injects unexpected gestures as if stepping in and out of a dream. A win for The Actor's Studio and a Blanche worth the trip downtown."

Previously unrecognized, the struggling actress was a stunning example of Studio method. Strangers stopped on the street to praise her performance, someone asked for an autograph. Free of doubt her posture changed. She was confident and spoke in an engaging voice. A door opened; Margerie became what she knew she could be.

30

Star-struck

An off-Broadway hit, *Streetcar Named Desire* sold out for a twelve-week run. After every performance friends and fans crowded backstage to pay tribute to the talented cast. Margerie's biggest surprise was the night Collie came towards her with Broadway legend Ravenna Pearl.

Critics raved about the spirited actress from the deep south, but it was outlandish behavior and a naughty wit that made her a popular celebrity. She only stayed for a minute. In an unmistakable husky voice, the celebrated star congratulated her then said with a chuckle, "Honey, for a Yankee girl you sure know a lot about Dixie!"

A month later they saw each other at a party. Ravenna asked her how she was, if there'd been prospects for another part, then graciously excused herself to join friends. Several drinks later she swept by, called her darling, and kissed a cheek. Then she asked if she lived alone. When Margerie said no, the glamorous star turned and stumbled into the night with two black lesbians.

31

Singing lesson

Even in New York nothing much happened in January. Todd called and said he was throwing a party. He lied. When Margerie arrived the only guests were an attractive young man and Ravenna Pearl. Greeting her like a long-lost friend, the leading lady made two vodka stingers and pulled her towards the couch.

"My dear little bird" Ravenna purred in a sultry voice, "so glad you made it. But look at you. So shy, reticent... that's the word, reticent! And why? There's no reason for it, none at all. Lift those wings and fly, soar up like an eagle!" And on she droned. "For God's sake you're not selling socks at Macy's. You're an actress so be one. Life darling... live it up. Live it up, love it up, and for God's sake drink it up!"

Resting a hand on her knee she waited for Margerie to comply. "Good girl, now we're both on empty. I'm driving the car dear, full speed ahead!" Jumping up to freshen their drinks her incessant blather continued. "Where the hell are those dirty boys? Guess Toddy got lucky with that Iowa bumpkin." The jaded star shared an insight. "Innocents dear, they're like eggs. You gotta get 'em while they're fresh."

Letting cigarette ash fall on the rug, Ravenna plowed back towards the couch. "Cozy up doll, here's your drinkie-poo." For a miraculous moment she paused. "Some party huh. Well c'est la vie darling, here's to us girls," and clinking glasses said, "C'mon now, do like those faggies do. Bottoms up!"

The wrath of vodka stingers lingered throughout the next day. Most of the night was foggy but one scene relentlessly flashed back. Barely conscious, she was sitting on the couch. The Queen of Broadway was on her knees, her head between Margerie's legs and pushing them apart. "Open up little bird," she slobbered, then raised the curtain. "Mama's gonna make you sing!"

32

Bang bang

Months went by without a word then he'd call. When Tony died and her mother passed, Daniel Drake sent elaborate floral sprays for the services. Now, if he was in Manhattan plugging a film or on a holiday, he'd take Margerie to an expensive restaurant and get V.I.P. seats for a Broadway show. Mercurial but loyal, her friendship with Daniel continued.

Browsing at the corner newsstand, she noticed him and two other Hollywood heartthrobs under a blazing headline on the cover of *Confidential*: "Can't Find A Girlfriend or Just Not Interested?" Knowing an expose could destroy his career she called to see how he was. Unflappable, Daniel thought it was funny but said his studio was not amused. "Publicity was on it as soon as they smelled blood," he said. "So they've teamed me up with that dyke Delores Hart. When we go out she brings a gal, I'm with a guy, we sit boy/girl at Mocambo and they take our picture. Call the columnists - Danny and Del double date! It's a riot Mar, make believe here never ends." When she asked if he was worried, he said, "Listen toots, I could leave here tomorrow and not give a shit. I stick around because I love the game."

Three months later he called again but sounded troubled. "Hey doll, it's Daniel. You better sit down. I'm going to say something you don't want to hear."

"I can tell." Ice cubes clinking in a glass meant he'd been drinking.

"There's no script so I'll cut to the chase. Mar's dead. That cowpoke husband shot her and her boyfriend. It was in today's L.A. Times."

He wasn't making sense. "Wait a minute. What are you talking about?"

"It's gruesome." Daniel paused and took another sip of bourbon. "The paper said around one in the morning Hank burst into the pool house and found Mar doing it with the chauffeur. Bang, bang, he shot 'em dead. It was on page two under a picture of her at a benefit for the Dallas Symphony."

"Oh my God" Margerie sighed. "I can't believe it."

"Well believe it girl, we both warned her. Whenever I told her to be discreet, she'd laugh and say I was jealous. Damn her! You two are the only women I care about." Choking up, Daniel had said enough. "Sorry, I can't talk about this anymore. I'll find out Texas protocol for murder and call you back."

She let him go. "Okay. At least I heard it from you. Take care."

Margerie felt disoriented, angry. Marianna called her last month, said she and Hank had been in France; loved the food, hated the French, and bought lots of clothes at Dior. Later she got a Chanel blouse Marianna sent from Paris.

A few days later Daniel called again. "Back to the wicked west. When I called Dallas a servant answered who barely spoke English. I tried being civil and asked where Mrs. Seebar was buried. "She's gone," she mumbled, "in urine now." Daniel paused. "I said, what? You mean her husband flushed her down the toilet?" The maid sounded confused and tried again. "No Mister, she at cemetery...in metal yurn." He laughed like he'd told a dirty joke and took another drink. "After that she told me Mr. Seebar was home from jail and sound asleep. So that's it, end of story. Case closed." Daniel said 'later gator' then hung up. There was no one else to mourn with.

Fiery, driven, and unapologetic about who she was, stunning beauty allowed Marianna to live her own version of la dolce vita. Nonetheless, she was a loyal and supportive friend. Thinking about forgiveness, Margerie wondered if her soul slipped into darkness or merged into light. Was manipulation to achieve wealth and pleasure a sin or did a distorted childhood foretell her future? Perhaps whatever allowed early abuse would forgive her folly. She hoped Marianna didn't suffer, died quickly in a flurry of bullets; that her friend was consumed in passion, held close in a lover's arms.

33

Goddess

Romantically linked to a New York playwright, Marilyn Monroe wanted to refine her acting. When she walked into The Actors Studio classmates pretended disinterest, but her presence was compelling: beauty and fame were intimidating.

Late for class she grabbed a seat next to Margerie then rummaging through her purse whispered, "Have you got a pen?" She smiled and gave her one.

About to leave at the end of class Marilyn said "Gee, I almost forgot," and handed the pen back. "What's your name?" she asked.

"Margerie" she answered. "Margerie Summers. Forget it, I've got tons of them."

"Okay then." Tying a scarf around her head she said, "Thanks Marge" before hurrying out. Nobody called her Marge; if they did, she corrected them. But it was Marilyn Monroe that said it. Sitting side by side they connected... maybe could grab a coffee, get to know each other, become friends. It made sense. Margerie was the kind of ally a famous star needed; Marilyn would appreciate sincerity, how trustworthy she was.

Waiting for a bus a few days later she saw Marilyn in a raincoat, wearing sunglasses. Getting into a cab she waved and yelled, "Hey Marge!" then drove off.

The next week the famous star sat on the other side of the room; a week later the founder started giving her private lessons. Even though a friendship never developed, Margerie worried about her. The destiny of a gentle soul seemed based on anatomy. Ravenous predators were closing in.

To satiate fans with gossip and photos, the press relentlessly followed her. Married, divorced, and remarried, she returned to Hollywood and got divorced again. A goddess in the midst of mortals, who could thwart what the world desired? Loved, used, and conflicted, Marilyn Monroe died six years later. Alone, naked, and cold to the touch; sprawled on an unmade bed.

THE 1960s

34

Sorry to hear that

In 1960, unable to afford an apartment, she took a room with bath on a week-to-week basis at the Dorsey Hotel. Assuming it was temporary, she stayed for 22 years.

A residential hotel on 28th street, the Dorsey had ten floors and 140 rooms. Behind each door there was someone on their way up, on their way down, or indifferent to where they'd landed. Clerks, theater people, and secretaries lived footsteps away from salesmen and retirees. A woman who'd sold lingerie at Gimbels lived on a pension but saw five movies a week. And every floor had someone who seemed content as long as a bar was nearby. The only thing that didn't change was people moving in or out.

An elderly man who lived down the hall stood next to her and waited for the elevator. Turning, Izaak Korczak smiled then introduced himself. His brown suit was worn like he was, but his eyes sparkled. Even so Margerie sensed lines on his face were trails of sorrow.

A few weeks later when a pair of shoes needed resoling, she walked to a shop she'd passed on the way to work. Inside she was surprised to see Mr. Korczak working on a boot. Calling his name he looked up, waved, then came over to see how he could help.

Margerie saw him a few weeks later feeding the squirrels in Madison Square. After saying hello she sat down. They talked about weather and their neighborhood then Izaak told her about his shop in Poland, how his family lived above the store. He showed her a picture taken in 1942. His wife Leeba and their daughter were sitting on a park bench just like they were. Three weeks later the Nazis sent them all to Treblinka; the women were killed but Izaak survived. After he put the photo back in his wallet, he took a peanut from a paper bag then made a clicking noise. A squirrel rushed over, set its tiny paws on Izaak's shoe then looked up. "This one's a friend," he said, "races over if he sees me." For an hour they sat together, watched leaves fall and dogs running in the square. Walking back to the Dorsey,

Mr. Korczak asked if her parents were living. When Margerie said no, he said he was sorry to hear that.

35

Survivor

A week later she saw Izaak in the hall. He asked her to wait so he could get something from his room then returned with a small box. Inside was a cloisonné brooch that belonged to his wife. Left with a gentile friend before going to a concentration camp, he retrieved it after the war. Now he gave it to her. Deeply touched she kissed his cheek then hurried off to work.

The following day before leaving for work, she wrote a note suggesting they meet for coffee. To make sure he'd see the message slipped under his door, she exposed a corner of the envelope. The next day it was still there. Two nights later when the white triangle was still visible, she sensed something was wrong.

No one had seen him. When she called the shoe repair shop whoever answered said he wasn't there and hung up. Fearing the worst, she got a manager and went to Izaak's room. The bed was made, clothes hung neatly in the closet, and everything looked orderly. Assuming he might be out of town the manager suggested they wait a few days before sounding an alarm.

Monday morning she insisted management call any reference Izaak gave when he moved in. They had one name but the number had been disconnected. Margerie called hospitals and filed a missing person report while police canvassed the morgues. A detective ventured a guess on what might've happened, but no one really knew. As allowed by law his things went into storage after thirty days. A young man studying modern dance rented the room a day later.

When she wore the brooch, if someone asked, she'd say it belonged to a Jewish woman who left it with a friend before being sent to a concentration camp. She'd tell them that Leeba and her daughter were killed by the Nazis but her husband survived, reclaimed the brooch after the war. Margerie would explain Mr. Korczak was a friend who lived down the hall, that he gave the pin to her. Compelled to finish, tears would fall; she'd say after handing her the gift, Izaak Korczak disappeared.

36

Segundo

Claire Dawes was a friend who gave up acting and married an advertising tycoon. Living large in a spacious apartment overlooking Union Square, she invited Margerie to their 10th anniversary party. After chatting a while with Claire, she didn't see anyone she knew so made her way to the buffet in the dining room. When someone next to her commented on the elaborate spread, she turned and looked into the eyes of a handsome man from Panama. After Segundo introduced himself, he mentioned he was a lighting technician at the Eugene O'Neil Theater.

"What a glorious place to work!" she said. "Have you seen *A Thousand Clowns*? I hear it's wonderful but impossible to get a ticket."

"Guess what?" His tan complexion complimented a bright smile. "I worked on the lighting from day one. It's a great production, you've gotta see it! Maybe I can get you a ticket."

Sitting down with plates on their laps they continued talking. She learned his wife had died and that a married son lived in Panama City. She told him where she was from, how long she'd been in the city, and how she knew Claire. Two hours seemed like twenty minutes. When they realized it was after midnight, Segundo insisted on walking her home.

Meeting for coffee a week later he surprised her with tickets for a matinee. After seeing the Broadway hit, they strolled through Central Park. Segundo revealed he was forty-one. He didn't ask and Margerie didn't tell she was pushing forty-seven.

When he discovered she'd never been there, he took her to Coney Island. They ate hot dogs, rode the Ferris wheel, then sat on a bench facing the ocean. He talked about Panama, fishing with his father in the Caribbean, and told stories that made her laugh. Segundo liked that. The next Sunday they held hands at a movie and he asked for a kiss. She'd forgotten what affection felt like. Dazzled and confused, she couldn't sleep.

Segundo invited her for dinner in his small, tidy apartment on East 26th Street. A bouquet of yellow tulips was on the table and after she sat down he gave her a kiss and glass of Rioja. Excusing himself, he went into the kitchen to check on the arroz con pollo.

After supper Segundo lit candles and they listened to Panamanian jazz. Pulling Margerie in close he kissed her again, then moaning slightly put a hand on her leg. Instinctively she resisted, shifted position and turned away. After an awkward silence he asked, "Am I going too fast? Did I do something wrong?"

She took a breath but couldn't face him. "Of course not. I didn't expect it…it's been a while. Even talking about it makes me uncomfortable."

Segundo took her hand. "You know there's no one else. The time we've spent together makes me happy. I told my son I met somebody and it's getting serious."

Calming down, she sounded sensible. "And you mean a lot to me. Maybe we should slow things down a little, wait a while."

Like a tortured young man, he explained himself. "I'm like my people. When I love someone, my body tells me. Reaching for you felt right. What I'm saying is I have my needs."

Anxious to leave Margerie feigned a headache. They walked out and Segundo hailed a cab. "Can I call tomorrow?" he asked. In a taxi with the window down she acted like nothing happened. "Of course darling, don't take this so seriously!" Then with a wave she was off.

She knew something had gone awry. Sex and intimacy seemed unfamiliar, complicated. The next day she didn't answer her phone. Segundo had opened her heart but she wouldn't lead him on. When he called again, she apologized, said she couldn't fulfill his needs and admitted it was her fault. His gentle voice sounded painful and it broke her heart. But what could she say? Ending their courtship, she could barely hear him. "God be with you," he whispered. Then the man from Panama hung up the phone.

37

Tony's hold

Even though Tony Regato was kind and thoughtful, it was his striking good looks that demanded attention. Maric marveled at his best friend's immunity to discord, how he connected to things without effort. Tony shared that world; without him nothing was the same.

Settling for a regulated life, Maric became a Lieutenant Colonel in the army and married an actress from Pasadena. Ten months later a baby girl arrived who later became a Hollywood star. Although he tried, his reserved nature inhibited closeness; that, plus the drinking, frustrated his wife. They divorced five years later.

Failing to succeed as an actress, Margerie struggled to make ends meet and questioned her worth. Incapable of bonding with another man, true love remained in historical territory. Tony was a hard act to follow.

Brother and sister held onto a space no one else could fill. Returning in dreams, Tony stayed long enough for them to suffer. But the pain was worth it. For a moment they relived the magic of Tony's hold.

38

Visualizing

A sordid night persistently flashed back; Margerie couldn't forget Ravenna Pearl slobbering between her legs. Drunk and incapacitated, she was too ashamed to tell anyone about what she considered sexual assault. For the first time, she hated someone.

Two years later the Broadway star literally bumped into her at the bar in Sardi's. Hanging onto the arm of British actor Burl Booth, Ravenna turned to greet her like an old friend but didn't remember her name.

"Margaret dear, you precious thing!" she gushed. "Burl darling, this is Margo. Margo Milkweed or something. Wonderful talent, Blanche Dubois... downtown stuff but sort of fabulous." Glancing off she quickly disengaged. "Oh God, there's Livy and Paul!" Tugging on her escort's arm she moved towards the glitterati. Feeling nauseous, Margerie asked the bartender for a glass of club soda.

A week later a piece in *Variety* reported Ravenna Pearl was flying to Hollywood for a screen test. After reading the news Margerie imagined a crashing plane; chaos and smoke, with no one injured but the Duchess of Drama. Fans would react to the shocking news. They'd say how cruel, ironic, what a terrible loss - celebrated actress loses her tongue! Visualizing her undoing was consoling: a pompous predator would leave the stage. Pearl's mouth would close, the silly babble would end. But best of all, without a tongue, what she did to her would be impossible.

39

Next President

When John Kennedy announced a run for president in 1960, he and his wife became symbols of the transformative decade to come. In spite of freezing weather, New York was hot for JFK.

Margerie landed a solid part in an off-Broadway play. Unfortunately, it couldn't compete with historic snow and closed after two performances. Downcast and discouraged, a friend surprised her with a ticket to *West Side Story*.

Better than the critics promised, the Broadway hit lifted her spirit; after the final curtain she happily made her way up the aisle. Flashbulbs going off in the lobby signaled a celebrity was creating a stir. Entering the crowd she glanced to her right and saw John Kennedy a few feet away. When someone stepped aside she charged in.

The youthful candidate from Massachusetts smiled at her. "Senator Kennedy," she beamed, "I'd like to shake the hand of our next President." He stooped down to thank her then kissed her cheek. Dazed, she looked at his handsome face then watched him move on.

Inspired by the encounter she joined his campaign and made calls urging people to vote for JFK. After he and Jackie moved into the White House, new energy surged across America. Three years later she was having a sandwich in a Greenwich Village coffee shop when a woman burst through the door. "They've shot Kennedy!" she screamed. "Somebody shot the President!" When the counterman turned on a radio horrid news poured out. Hoping for a miracle she rushed home, but JFK was dead. After listening to the painful details, she finally dozed off. The gruesome saga continued without her.

The next day she sought refuge in an old Catholic church. Looming over 23rd street like a weary sentry, tall buildings compromised light trying to reach the vaulted ceiling. In the dim cathedral she watched an elderly Black man light a candle beneath Mary's outstretched arms. At the front of the church, two Spanish women on their knees looked up at Jesus like they expected him to say something. A few rows ahead a woman with a small boy trembled as she sobbed. Hoping to comfort his mother her son stood up on the pew, reached over, and put his tiny hands on her head.

Margerie remembered Kennedy standing in the crowded lobby, how he smiled, kissed a cheek, and lifted her spirit during a troubling time. Now in shadowed space, she found refuge in the company of saints. Joining strangers, she sat there and wept.

40

Alterations

The lining in her winter coat fell apart. She overheard someone in the hotel coffee shop say, "Ray Ginetti isn't very nice but he's a damn good tailor." Later she saw his card on the hotel bulletin board - Ginetti Design & Alterations, Suite 207, The Dorsey Hotel.

Margerie had nothing to lose so took her coat and knocked on the door of his two-room suite. "I hear you," said a disgruntled voice. "The door's open, try turning the knob." In a room crowded with bolts of material and racks of clothes, Ray Ginetti sat hunched over his sewing machine.

"Hold on, I gotta finish this seam." A minute later he looked up. "So what ya got?

Stepping forward she handed him her winter coat. "As you can see Mr. Ginetti the lining…"

He quickly interrupted. "Ray, call me Ray. Mister sounds old. Do I look old?" He took the coat and gave it a look. "Cheap lining, probably from Japan. Everything they make is junk. The coat looks okay and it's not very big so twenty bucks. You pick, red or black?"

She told him black was okay and he prattled on. "I've seen you in the lobby. You don't look like the rest of the herd. What do you do?"

"I'm an actress," she said. "And I do some private coaching."

"Oh yah, how's that working?" he said sarcastically. "You're in a tough racket. Theater, entertainment…after a certain age you're toast. I had an aunt, she was a singer and pretty good too. After she turned forty no one was interested, including men. I told her she shoulda grabbed a guy when she looked good. She's got a cat now and lives in Hoboken. How tall are you?"

Hoping he'd do a good job on the coat she tried being pleasant. "I guess I'm a petite, five-foot-four."

"Well, Tiny, we got that in common. I'm five five and hate it. Us shrimps go to the end of the line." He had another question. "What's your name again?"

"Margerie." she said. "Margerie Summers."

"Sounds show-bizzy." Pausing a moment, he returned to his sewing. "Sorry, no more chitchat. I'm one of those people that's gotta work. So ten on deposit, ten due, ten days you pick it up. Ten-ten-ten. I make it easy for the dumbos around here."

Anxious to leave his toxic domain she handed him the money. "Okay Ray, see you then." But Ginetti had the last word. "Not if I see you first."

When she picked up her coat she left as quickly as possible. Examining it back in her room she was impressed, the relining was perfect. Regardless of his negative disposition he'd done a great job.

Two weeks later she got home late after stopping at the Madison bar. Someone wearing a motorcycle jacket was waiting for the elevator. She got in, pushed a button, then turned around; it was Ray Ginetti. Reeking of alcohol and judging by a sullen expression and swollen eye, she figured he'd been roughed up. Just to say something she said, "Good evening."

"You think so?" he snarled. "what's good about it? And don't be checking me out. Look in a mirror Tiny. You don't look so hot either."

Taken aback she said, "I didn't mean to…" but Ray shut her down.

"Did, didn't, who gives a shit? It's late so stuff it. At least I got my rocks off."

The door opened on the second floor. "Okay Broadway" he slurred, "you know what they say, break your leg." Snickering, he got out and weaved towards his two-room suite.

41

Tickets please

Nothing paid off. Despite the effort, Margerie had only landed three small parts in three years. Barely staying afloat, she had few options so got a job ushering in the Shubert Theaters.

Taking tickets from people she knew was embarrassing, and every theater fanatic showed up to see *Bye Bye Birdie*. For those surprised to see her in uniform, she had a comeback. "You know show biz. Curtain up, curtain down. But I'll be back!" Her routines varied. "I'm training for a part…seasoned actress hits the skids." Margerie got a few laughs and some tips, but it was humiliating. She took a shot of vodka before putting on her usher's jacket.

It was a busy Thursday night and most of the house was seated. Across the lobby she noticed a platinum blonde in sunglasses rushing towards her station with an older man. Wearing a long sable coat, she thought it was Hollywood starlet Mamie Van Doren. Before she could say tickets please, the flashy bombshell froze in place. "Oh my God, I don't believe it!" and lifting her sunglasses said, "Miss Summers, is that you?"

Under make-up and fur stood Daisy Cieplak, the teenage tramp of Jamestown. Turning towards her escort she said, "Harry, this lady was my dancing teacher back home!" Bending down Daisy gave her a big hug. Smiling awkwardly Miss Summers said she was glad to see her but had to seat them before the lights went down.

After final curtain Margerie stood at her station by the door. One of the last to leave, Daisy stopped to chat with her former coach. "Harry, I'll meet you outside. I want to say goodbye to Miss Summers." Staring down from her high-heeled perch, Daisy picked up where she left off. "I can't wait to tell Mom! Small world Miss Summers... what's it been, twenty years?"

"Just about." She changed the subject. "And what about you dear, do you live here now?"

"You bet. Been here four years and I love it. I was married you know. Got divorced but was lucky, no kids to worry about. I got out of Hicksville fast, did some modeling and stuff and have a place on Park Avenue."

Hoping their reunion would end, Margerie remained polite. "That sounds nice."

For a few moments Daisy said nothing. "Gee Miss Summers, I don't want to sound nosy, but how did you end up doing this?"

"It's just temporary dear," she answered. "Acting is unpredictable, you've got to roll with the punches."

"I guess you're right," Daisy figured, then reached out to put something in her teacher's hand. "Listen, it was great seeing you. Take this."

She glanced at a hundred-dollar bill. "Oh, Daisy. No, I couldn't."

"Sure you can. Now put it in your pocket." Daisy smiled. "Trust me," she insisted, "to Harry it's like dropping a dime." Another hug and she was off. "I gotta run now Miss Summers. See ya around!"

Daisy's perfume lingered. She knew it was expensive. Walking away, she watched her sable coat sway majestically from side to side. Margerie imagined Harry waiting in a limousine, ready to take her former student to a plush Manhattan club. Leaning against a wall she looked around the empty theater and saw the janitor lock the front door. Everyone had left.

42

Mateo

Every Sunday if the weather was good she walked to Perez Produce to pick up some fruit, almonds, maybe a bag of banana chips. One afternoon Mr. Perez introduced her to his fourteen-year-old son. He was helping his dad stack fruit. When she picked up a melon Mateo smiled and asked to see it; shook the cantaloupe and said there was a better one in back. He returned a few minutes later looking like he'd found gold. "This one's a winner," he beamed. "Young man," she said, "so are you." He laughed and a friendship started.

In Manhattan she rarely had a chance to interact with younger people. Now Mateo smiled the moment he saw her. It was uplifting. Kind and curious, he'd never met an actress before. Margerie's sincere interest in who he was made him feel good. Age didn't matter, they had a special friendship.

On a summer day when the store was empty, she saw him sitting on a box sketching something. He was fifteen and they were buddies, so she asked to see what it was. Surprised to see a meticulous drawing of customers selecting fruit and vegetables, Margerie said, "Oh my, I had no idea you were an artist." Mateo waited a moment then asked, "Do you think it's any good?"

"Good?" she answered. "No. It's outstanding! For a change you're going to see me speechless."

As she continued to study the drawing he said "I've got more at home, maybe I'll bring some in. And I've started painting."

"I'm overwhelmed," she said. "What a surprise, I'd love to see them! And I'm not just saying that. You've got a special talent."

His brown eyes looked so innocent he could've been an angel. "Miss Summers, what you say means a lot to me." Then he stood up. "Can I give you a hug?"

The next weekend she saw more drawings and deeply impressed, dropped by on Tuesday to tell Mr. Perez how talented his son was. Grinning, he sighed. "I know. What am I gonna do? It's not very practical being an artist but he's a good boy. I gotta let him do what he wants." Handing her a box of strawberries he said, "On the house. Mateo says you inspire him. So thank you."

It was true, she did. Searching through a used book store she found a portfolio of color prints by Caravaggio, Botticelli, and Titian. It wasn't cheap but she didn't care, wrapped it in red paper, then gave it to him just before Christmas. Over and over he told her it was his favorite book and made sure she was up to date on what he was painting in high school.

His senior year, Margerie went to see two of Mateo's paintings on display at a young artists exhibition at Brooklyn's Borough Hall. Figurative and bold, she was amazed. Mrs. Perez took a picture of her and Mateo standing by his painting. Tall now, slender and sensuous-looking, he was too good-looking according to his mother. When girls called on school nights, she'd tell them he was busy doing homework and to call on the weekend. Graduating in 1965, Margerie treated him to an exhibition of paintings by Picasso and Vincent Van Gogh at the Metropolitan Museum.

Mateo wanted to go to Pratt or The School of Visual Arts. Expensive choices, he decided to work for a year to make tuition and got a job unloading trucks for a produce distributor. It made sense. He could save money and live at home.

Sharing his future was a delight. Margerie remembered talking with Tony, how they both wanted children. He said six, then teased her, said he'd settle for five. When she told him she'd stop at four, he said, "What do you mean? Stop what?" and they laughed. She considered her friendship with Mateo a gift from God. They talked on the phone, went to galleries together, and she took him to his first Broadway musical. Feeling loved and helpful, whatever brought them together was a blessing.

43

Vietnam

After a long tour of duty in Viet Nam, Lt. Colonel Maric Summers came back damaged. He'd seen 23 men killed, lost a finger, was deaf in one ear, and suffered from "battle fatigue." Confined in a V.A. hospital, Margerie scraped together the money and flew to California to see her brother.

Robbed of independence, Maric languished in an overcrowded, understaffed facility. Drinking coffee from a vending machine, his second wife told Margerie that her brother couldn't sleep and begged to go home. Surrounded by casualties she saw what the government tried to hide: hell reigned in Viet Nam.

It was 1967. Impatience, disillusionment, and anger fed a cultural revolution. Long-haired rebels roamed the streets, alternative newspapers encouraged protest, and unabashed hippies asked for change. The day she got back to New York a girl in sandals, bell bottoms and a peasant blouse, gave her a flower at the airport. A free spirit from Kansas, she told Margerie she lived in the East Village and was selling peace buttons. Margerie bought one and pinned it on.

A day later she walked to her favorite produce store. Behind his cash register, Mr. Perez wasn't smiling. "Did Mateo call you?" he asked.

"He might have," she answered. "I've been in California and just got back."

"Well he will, a bomb dropped. He got a draft notice last week."

"What?" She froze.

"He's going for his physical next week."

Feeling faint she sat on a produce box. "Good lord, he just turned nineteen."

"They don't care. If he was in college they couldn't touch him, he'd get a deferment. It's not like he's loafing around. My brother knows somebody on the city council, is going to see him tomorrow. Maybe he'll help. My wife's going crazy."

She tried calming down. "I can't believe I'm hearing this. How's Mateo doing?"

"You know my son; he goes with the flow while the rest of us freak out."

Margerie met Mateo for coffee. With youthful bravado he acted more surprised than upset, said a friend got a draft notice the same day he did. "Who knows, it might work out," he told her. "Maybe the army will pay for college when I get back." Sensing he was being nonchalant to reassure her, she didn't reveal her deep concern.

A month later Mrs. Perez invited her to a send-off party on a Saturday night so she took a subway to Brooklyn. All smiles, Mateo greeted her with a big hug. "Tonight we party, so no sad faces," he told her. "Pretend you're Puerto Rican!" In spite of Latin salsa, rum and dancing, she was on the verge of tears all night. A few days later war claimed another man she loved; Mateo left for boot camp.

44

Absence of light

It was the middle of March. Overcast and cold, the promise of Spring had yet to come. He'd been a soldier for five months. She prayed for him every day.

After filling in for Rose at a Wednesday matinee, she went to pick up some fruit at Perez Produce. When she got there it was closed. A piece of paper taped on the door had something written with a black marker; in bold letters it got right to the point. 'PVT. MATEO PEREZ - K.I.A. Services Pending.'

It couldn't be true. Margerie read it again and again. Her heart started pounding; she leaned against the building. Someone would've called she thought, but maybe I wasn't home. Running around for two days, she hadn't checked to see if she'd gotten any messages. Her watch said ten after four, the store closed at seven. She didn't move. It took a few minutes for her to realize the worst had happened.

Heaviness filling her body felt familiar. Crossing 23rd street, she sat on a bench at the edge of Madison Square. Three weeks earlier she sent Mateo a group of postcards, paintings by Diego Rivera. She wondered if he got them. Margerie thought about his beautiful hands, the innocence in his eyes, how he smiled. He was just a boy. Her boy. Young, happy, and full of life. Talented. She sat there crying.

Wet with tears Margerie's handkerchief looked like a rag. Cars, trucks, and people going home hurried by. When a dog stopped to sniff her shoes the woman holding a leash smiled and said it was getting windy. She looked at her, said nothing, stared at the produce store across the street.

Where was he when it happened, was anyone there to hold him? Did someone take him in their arms, tell Mateo he'd be okay even if it wasn't true? She thought about his family in Brooklyn: brothers, sisters, his best friend Rego. Maybe seeing the note was better than making his father tell me on the phone. Why did it happen, what's the point? Anger distracted her. It was cold but she sat there until it got dark. Only an absence of light gave her the strength to walk back to her room.

On April 15th, 1967, the day before his 20th birthday, she pinned a peace button on her coat and joined 800,000 people filling the Manhattan streets. Every sort of person came to protest: rebels, rabbis, widows, doctors, and veterans, walked beside students and someone's parents. They came from every state and demanded an end to war. Everyone had a reason; Margerie had three. Mateo Perez, Tony Regato and Maric Summers.

45

Sunday

All afternoon it rained. She fell asleep reading a magazine then awakened by thunder, opened her eyes. Margerie had no idea where she was. A wooden bureau, metal floor lamp, the radio, books, clothes on a chair...everything surrounding her seemed unfamiliar. Getting off the bed she looked out the window but nothing, inside or out, made sense.

The disorientation lasted for several minutes. Then slowly, like pieces in a jigsaw puzzle, cognition slowly reassembled.

Later, soaking in a hot tub, she stared at black and white tiles as her muscles relaxed. Being lost in a jumble was of no concern; the familiar as an unknown did not alarm her. It was the peace in detachment she thought about as the water chilled.

46

April 4th, 1968

She'd seen racism in Texas, Illinois, Florida, and Hollywood. Tony told her about prejudice in the military, how Negro men ready to die for their country were segregated. When Martin Luther King stepped forward things happened; America was listening.

Adelae, a maid at the Dorsey Hotel, came by twice a month with sheets and towels. Happy to hear a knock on her door, Margerie always had pastry or a chocolate bar waiting. For eight years they talked about the news, weather, families, and faith. Every birthday she gave Addie earrings and after hearing her sing in a Harlem choir, bought her Marian Anderson's autobiography.

Winter had faded, bright sunlight revealed hints of Spring. But that Thursday she woke up feeling apprehensive; all day she felt uneasy.

Before opening the theater doors that evening, the house manager summoned his ushers into the lobby. He had horrible news. "Martin Luther King has been killed in Memphis." Gasps and murmurs filled the room. "People will be arriving soon and some of them won't know what's happened. There'll be an announcement and the show will go on. Please take a moment of silence for this extraordinary man."

Stonewalling grief, she did her job. By the time she left the theater Times Square had closed down. Sirens pierced the night as fire engines raced to wherever rage turned into flames. The subway was deserted, people sheltered in place, and no one knew what would happen.

In 1963 she taped part of King's speech in Washington on her mirror; it was still there. "In spite of the difficulties and frustrations of the moment, I still have a dream." In 1965, to support Black Americans, Margerie donated a week's salary for his march in Selma. Collaborating raised her spirit; she was hopeful, optimistic. Now she felt disillusioned and depressed.

At the Dorsey, management moved a television into the lobby. Sitting with a silent group Margerie heard tributes for a leader who was alive seven hours earlier. Riots and looting exploded across the country. Warned not to go before an angry crowd in Indianapolis, Robert Kennedy went anyway.

Opening his heart, he asked the anguished to honor Dr. King with non-violence; they listened and dispersed in tears. She'd seen enough and went to her room. It was a sleepless night.

At noon the next day Addie knocked on her door holding sheets and towels. "You shouldn't be here" Margerie said. "I don't know how you can function." When she stepped in, they hugged each other.

Adelae sat on the bed. "It's crazy uptown. Trash all over, windows broken… we got so much smoke no one can breathe. I had to get outta there, figured I might as well come to work." Margerie made tea on the hotplate as she continued. "Tonight I'll go to church. Tyrone's taking me and Edna Donald over. She's ninety but spry as can be…lives next door with her cat." For a minute neither of them spoke. "I got to wonder what's the use. Every Sunday I pray hard... protect this man, you keep Martin safe Jesus. Last night mama calls and says, 'Addie, I guess I won't get to see it. Not in my lifetime. Dr. King's gone to the promised land.'

Margerie turned off the heat under the kettle and started crying. "Oh Addie… what's happening? It doesn't make sense to me, God, or anyone else."

"I know. But now what?" Addie took a sip of tea. "The young bloods are fed up. They've heard it all, seen it all, and want to burn everything down. They're mad and I don't blame 'em. We waited a long time for Martin. Now me, mama, us older ones, we're bone tired... the light's gone out." Tears rolling down her white friend's face signaled hope. Getting up she put a hand on Margerie's shoulder. "Maybe after we bury him people won't forget. Maybe that dream Martin had will be like he said. We won't see color... we'll climb that mountain together."

47

Elaine Reilly

Elaine Reilly was third generation. Both sets of grandparents came from Ireland and settled in Akron, Ohio. Fifteen when her mother died, taking care of things was her responsibility.

Slender and Irish pretty, auburn hair framed a face as white as porcelain. Too busy to lollygag on the street or in high school corridors, Elaine focused on what had to be done at home. Conversations were succinct and she got straight to the point. Her smile looked fabricated, polite but cautionary, like she was prepared to defend herself. Her only friend, an older cousin, moved to Kentucky and became a nun. Homework, housekeeping, and solitude dominated Elaine's teenage life.

A manager at a Firestone tire plant, her father barely functioned without his wife. On Saturdays Mike

Reilly worked in the yard, watched sports, and drank beer. On Sunday morning he went to an early mass by himself. Grateful but reserved, he'd tell Elaine she was a "good girl" and occasionally brought home pastries or Chinese takeout. When her brother left for college, Elaine got a secretarial job and continued her role at home.

Thirty-one when her Father died, she'd never been east of Ohio. Tired of being uncomfortable with who she was, Elaine surprised everyone by announcing a move to New York City. It wasn't for fame or fortune, to design or sing, but to escape a world of football weekends, church suppers, and married with children. Magazines, books, and movies led her to believe she belonged in Manhattan. Her brother called it a reckless choice and predicted the massive metropolis would eat her alive. Even that seemed appealing. Confident she'd find a job, she refused to alter her plan.

After her train arrived at Grand Central, she took a cab to the Martha Washington Hotel. When they said they had no record of a reservation Elaine remained remarkably calm. An apologetic manager made a phone call, then recommended the Dorsey Hotel three blocks away. She picked up her bags and started walking.

Every kind of person rushed by in different directions; all of them looking like they were on a serious mission. Passing a newsstand, she saw food carts selling frankfurters and shish kabobs, then someone asked if she wanted to buy a watch. Navigating around stacks of merchandise on the sidewalk, she stopped on a corner and watched truck drivers yell at a bicycle messenger weaving between them like a snake. Horns honked, traffic jammed, and sirens wailed in the distance. Elaine smiled; being in the midst of New York's legendary ruckus felt marvelous.

Turning the corner on 28th street, the Dorsey Hotel came into view. A friendly clerk at the front desk said he had a sunny room on a residential floor then asked if she was an actress. She blushed, said no, but considered it flattering. Facing the street, the sixth-floor room had a bed, bureau, desk, new rug and upholstered chair. A final surprise, the spotless bathroom had an enormous tub.

She unpacked, fell on the bed, and stared at the ceiling. Life in Akron had drained her one drop at a time; glad to be gone, doubts surfaced anyway. She didn't know anyone or where anything was. What had she done? Maybe her brother was right, it was an impulsive move. Starting to shiver, Elaine felt like she was under a silk sheet; something shiny, appealing, but impractical. Tired and confused she dozed off in tears.

When she woke up it was 5:30. People were heading home after work. Elaine listened to the rhythm of Manhattan and knew her heart was beating with one-and-a-half million others on a concrete slab. One of them, a woman in the Dorsey Hotel, would be there to help.

48

Chance meeting.

Margerie knew things changed if she did. Overcoming draining situations took discipline, motivation, and faith. Once again, she focused on metaphysics and maintaining a positive perspective. It wasn't easy but it worked; for the time being her demons were at rest. A cheerful disposition, interest in others, and passion for all things creative, returned.

On an ordinary morning she sensed a new cycle was starting. Taking the subway to Times Square, she checked usher assignments at the Shubert, picked up *Variety*, then stopped for a hot dog at Nathan's. After getting vitamin C, calcium tablets and a protein bar, she started home.

Back on 28th Street it was pouring rain. A young woman she'd seen in the lobby had taken refuge under an awning so Margerie introduced herself then offered to share an umbrella. Surprised, Elaine Reilly thanked her, and huddled together they hurried back to the hotel. Later they met for dinner.

In spite of twenty-six-years difference in age, they bonded. An unlikely pairing, they became as close to each other as they'd been to anyone. A loner from Akron, who'd found the Dorsey by chance, partnered with someone accustomed to change. From the beginning they accepted each other's flaws and got what they needed: comfort, support. and unconditional love.

49

June 6, 1968

Margerie overslept; it was after ten and her appointment at Bancroft Beauty School was for 11:30. She showered, got dressed, did make-up, then raced to the subway.

The only seat was beside two long-haired hippies who reeked of marijuana and patchouli. The guy next to her seemed dazed but his friend looked serious. Facing his buddy he sounded upset.

"Shit, another bummer. I can't believe somebody popped Bobby."

The clueless one sounded puzzled. "Oh yeah. Bobby who?"

"Kennedy man, Bobby Kennedy! He was out there in L.A."

"L.A. bro… that's a crazy town," he said. "I hitched out there last year. Who did him in, the pigs?"

"No man, the fucking cops were asleep! Some asshole shot him in the kitchen."

The stoner turned and looked at Margerie. "Wow. How fucked up is that?"

Getting off at Times Square she grabbed a paper, leaned against a lamppost, and let continuing bad news sink in. She had an appointment, was filling in for Rose at a matinee, and had to focus on things at hand. She'd deal with emotion later.

A student at beauty school asked about hair color. "Blonde." she said. "Not platinum, something bright. Like champagne." Margerie tried to block what raced through her head. Robert Kennedy. Why him? They're killing the good guys! Hoping to bypass invasive thoughts, she kept talking. "And dear, the color has got to cover. You know how dreary gray is, it creeps in." She paused then continued. "I can't figure it out. I find something I like but it never lasts. It's perfect then the color turns on you... is gone, just like that."

50

Helen's party

Her best friend in high school came from Jamestown's richest family. After graduating from Sarah Lawrence, Helen Thorpe married a Harvard man named Sam and moved to Connecticut. After their kids grew up Helen and Sam bought a luxurious brownstone on East Sixty-Third. Every year they invited Margerie to a lavish party after the holidays.

Still in a room at the Dorsey Hotel, February 1969 was rough. After a Broadway show closed the ushers got laid off; then her only elocution student moved to the West Coast. When Helen called to remind her of the upcoming party, she said Sam booked a gypsy band and their son was coming in from Dartmouth. Sounding enthused Margerie promised to be there, but after the call felt worse; stayed in bed, ate peanut butter, and listened to the radio.

Whenever she felt really miserable, Margerie ran into Ray Ginetti. Unfortunately, she converged with his dark aura at the front desk while getting her mail. Casually he asked how she was and recklessly she told him. "Not great. Things are pretty tight." Ray cued up and let go like a loose bowel. "Face it, Margo," he sneered, "it's time you woke up. You've been in the dumps for years. Kiss those dreams of yours goodbye and get a real job like the rest of us."

The night of the party she tried being optimistic. Putting on a black dress she'd worn the year before, she dressed it up with a turquoise scarf Daniel Drake sent at Christmas. It looked expensive and someone might notice; if so, she could say it was from her darling friend, the Hollywood star. Ready to put on shoes, it suddenly registered her best high heels were being re-soled. Frantically she searched for another pair.

Margerie knew how the evening would unfold. The women would be chatty, self-assured graduates from prestigious schools who married wealthy men. Their husbands would be polite but boring. She'd be the novelty guest, a spunky actress from Helen's hometown. Even though her performance in *Streetcar Named Desire* was 16 years ago, she'd be introduced as "the best Blanche Dubois ever." That said, Margerie would slip into character and pretend to lead a fulfilling theatrical life.

Leaving the Dorsey in horrible weather, she opened her umbrella, stepped into slush, and trudged towards the subway. Loosen up she thought; consider the benefits, have some fun. Think of this as a reprieve... the food will be good, they'll have live music, and after a few drinks you can relax. And besides, Sam will insist on paying for a cab home.

Two blocks later she felt unsteady, her foot wobbled. When a heel broke off optimism went with it and the curtain fell. Face it she thought, Ray Ginetti was right. You're a dreamer, flop, a has-been who never was. But keep smiling... stand strong, do your act. The show must go on.

Her foot was soaking wet. When she bent down to pick up the heel she boiled over. Are you kidding, what am I doing? Look at yourself. Why bother? To hell with Helen and Sam, their gypsy band and cold lobster... I'm not going. Who cares what they think! Helen doesn't have a clue how things are. Turning around in a rage, she stepped off the curb and a taxi screeched to a halt. Inches away, the cabbie punched his horn, rolled down a window, and yelled. Eager to engage an enemy, Margerie threw the heel at his windshield like a hand grenade.

"You piece of shit!" she screamed, then slammed her umbrella against his hood. "Wake the fuck up!"

Glaring like a deranged savage she stood in his headlights and flipped him the finger. "Go to hell you moron. You almost ran me over!"

Thirty-five blocks from the dazzle of Helen's party a weary warrior fought the elements. Head down, with no umbrella, she hobbled back to her room.

51

Falling down

Disappointments led to depression. Counsel and perseverance required effort; worn out, she yielded to apathy.

Being short on money didn't stop her from late night drinking. A few cocktails were an escape from reality and induced long periods of sleep. Tony, her mother, Mateo, and others, appeared in dreams unconnected to a dismal life. Fifty-four, Margerie looked ten years younger, but a mutation slipped in. An actress who recognized variations, she saw it reflected on plate glass windows and towering mirrors at Macy's. Anxiety and discouragement altered her demeanor; even her voice sounded frayed and apprehensive.

Over the years she nurtured the notion that March was an unlucky month. It was no surprise when a fierce gust of wind knocked her down on West Forty-Fifth street. Dropping a notebook, she helplessly watched all of her papers tumble towards Eighth Avenue. A yellow scarf ripped from her neck flew off like a crazed bird while things from her purse rolled into the gutter. Lying on the sidewalk, someone offered help but she didn't respond. Closing her eyes she pulled her legs to her chest and stayed in a fetal position.

Margerie barely remembered what happened. Waking up in a sterile room she asked someone in a uniform where she was. "You're in Bellevue," the nurse said. "It's your nerves."

52

Protector

The end of April was warm and sunny so Elaine thought an afternoon in Madison Square would lift Margerie's spirit. After buying two coffees and a Sunday Times, she walked with her friend to their neighborhood park.

They found a bench in a quiet spot and began to unwind. Unfortunately, their peaceful interlude was interrupted when three boys ran into the park and started knocking over barrels of trash. Racing towards them with screams and laughter, Margerie gave the ringleader a disapproving look. Acknowledging her reproach, he stopped and faced her.

"What you lookin' at lady?"

The lady answered. "What I'm looking at young man, is garbage all over the walk," then cautiously added, "and really dear, on such a beautiful day."

Hesitating he bounced back, then waving a stick began a tirade. "You got somethin' better to look at? You got somethin' under that dress grandma?" The other boys cheered him on and the harassment escalated. "C'mon now, tell me about it. You lose your voice? What you got under there?"

Tucking her dress under her legs, Margerie froze. Elaine said nothing, put down the newspaper and stared at the junior thug.

"You hear me bitch? Now you all quiet. You guys wanna see?" and with their encouragement poked his stick at the hem of her dress.

Suddenly Elaine jumped up, reached out and grabbed the boy's head. Holding his wiry hair in hand, she shook him and yelled, "Listen to me you little monster, don't you touch her! Do you understand?" When the boy freed himself and ran off Elaine's auburn hair flamed in the sun. Standing strong, she raised a closed Irish fist. "Do you hear me?" she screamed. then warned him again. "Just don't you dare!"

THE 1970s

53

Tribal privilege

People came to New York with every kind of hope. A city of dreams and demolition, things impossible anywhere else happened here. When Margerie was cast as Blanche Dubois, the older sister in *Streetcar Named Desire*, she was already thirty-six. Unfortunately, persistence and talent weren't enough; she never made it to Broadway. Even so, she belonged in Manhattan and intended on staying.

Rich, poor, notable or not, everyone shared the streets and subways. Native New Yorkers said what they thought and if it bothered you, they didn't care. Anyone living there long enough inherited a tribal privilege: don't let anyone push you around.

Rats, roaches, dirty streets and incessant noise, drove people crazy. But even in a blizzard you could grab a cab, take a train, and get anywhere in the five boroughs 24/7. Theaters, restaurants, and museums were only part of it; sex and money kept the city spinning. Distractions made it difficult to focus on ethereal things, but most people didn't care. New York was addictive and beyond city limits the high disappeared; if you returned the hallucinogen kicked in anew.

Margerie offered support and recognition to everyone she knew. Even though her dreams didn't materialize, she was a colorful character who belonged in a creative and stimulating place. Uptown, Downtown, East or West side, in Manhattan she could simply be who she was.

54

Roommate relief

Margerie felt safe in the Dorsey Hotel until an elderly man in the room next door began harassing her. After midnight, she was in bed when he started furiously knocking on the wall between them. She called the desk, heard the phone in his room ring, and the knocking stopped. Two nights later as she fumbled for a key his door swung open. Standing in pajamas he hissed at her like an angry cat. After that, every night a snorting pig, howling wolf, or lion's roar, was waiting when she reached her door. When management failed to stop animal threats from the room next door, Margerie called the police.

After re-enacting the drama for a rookie cop in the Dorsey lobby, he escorted her to the seventh floor. Finding a mild-mannered senior instead of the lunatic described, he entered his room and closed the door. Ten minutes later the officer came out and assured her there would be no more trouble.

The cacophony stopped but fierce knocking on the wall resumed. Demanding to be moved, management said that they had nothing available but could put a roll-away bed in Elaine's room until the problem was resolved.

Every night was like a slumber party; they drank chamomile tea, ate chocolates, chattered, and laughed like schoolgirls. Getting in bed she waited for Elaine to shut off the lights, then turned on her side ready to sleep. For two weeks she felt cheerful and protected; the way she did before Tony died.

55

Drop me off

She'd known Bruce Cabot for years. A casual acquaintance and wealthy patron of the arts, Margerie ran into him at a memorial service for a mutual friend. When he asked her to join him for dinner, she hesitated but Cabot insisted. Moments later they rode off in his black limousine.

After a splendid meal in a French bistro, the chauffeur dropped Cabot off in Carnegie Hill and was about to take Margerie home when she had an idea. "Oh, James… I hope it's no bother, but I just remembered a promise I made to meet some people at Charlie's. Do you know where it is?"

"Yes Ma'am, on West Forty-Sixth. No problem at all. I'll just cut through the park."

There were no promises and no one was waiting, but Charlie's would be packed and she could make a spectacular entrance. After freshening her makeup, she adjusted a mink turban from Union Thrift then savored the ride through Central Park.

James maneuvered the stretch-Cadillac so its passenger door was in front of the restaurant awning. Before she got out she saw actress Olive Reed sitting by a window staring at the car. A malicious drinker, she once introduced Margerie to a famous playwright as "Dear little Mags, everyone's favorite usher."

The chauffeur opened the door and reached for her hand. With the poise of a seasoned royal she said, "Thank you James," then stepping out glanced at Olive's stunned reaction. Joining a lively group at the bar Margerie ordered a glass of pink champagne and topping it off, ordered another.

She'd spent the money kept in her bra. Unable to afford a cab, she walked to the subway, put a token in the slot, then replayed a marvelous night. First was dinner with Bruce: the escargot, coq au vin, and a remarkable cabernet. Then it was cruising through town in a luxurious limousine. But the best part was her entrance; how James opened the door, took her hand as she stepped out. It was the precise moment she saw that astonished look on the face of dreadful Olive Reed.

56

Always a reason

After losing Tony, then their mother, the bond between Maric and Margerie grew stronger. Eager to be a doting aunt for her brother's daughter, she made two trips to the West Coast to visit Katie. Unfortunately, her mother filed for divorce five years later. Visits with her niece became few and far between.

Acting since middle school, Katie Summers was a natural. Landing a part in a television sit-com at twelve, she soon had a part in a feature film. Aunt Margerie sent reviews and clippings to keep her informed on what was happening in New York. Proudly watching her niece's meteoric ascent, she wasn't surprised that Katie won an Academy Award when she was 25.

During a visit with Maric in California, Margerie

was invited to spend a weekend at Katie's luxurious house in Brentwood. A year later, when Katie was in New York, they spent an afternoon together. There was a picture of them having lunch on the celebrity wall at Joe Allen's.

Katie sent her aunt a gift on Christmas and birthdays, but what Margerie treasured was her phenomenal success. Recognition that eluded her now came through her niece. In the hotel lobby or at work, in a bar, restaurant, or wherever there was an opportunity, she had updates on the Hollywood star. Relevance didn't matter; there was always a reason to bring up Katie.

57

Psychic input

Daughter of a Russian staret, Malvina Barkov claimed she had lived in Tibet and studied with Krishnamurti in India. A blunt "intuitive," Madam Barkov's observations were reputed to be life changing. Montgomery Clift had seen her, so had Marilyn Monroe. After a single session Collie Berg quit his job as a director at Actor's Studio. Barkov didn't mince words. She told him he was wasting his time in New York; the money was in Hollywood. He left for the West Coast two weeks later.

Margerie rarely complained but failed ambition, a nominal income, and the effects of aging, were agonizing. She'd studied metaphysics, the Kabbalah, dabbled in Silva Mind Control, and spiritual regression. But it wasn't enough. Maybe this clairvoyant could guide her. She borrowed money and made an appointment.

Two weeks later in a vintage building on Riverside Drive, an assistant said Madam Barkov would see her. Inside a room full of baroque furniture and shadowy paintings, tapestry curtains blocked sunlight from coming through the windows. Nonetheless Malvina was highly visible behind her desk. Dyed black hair framed a sagging face that looked tired of saving the world. Only her arms, adorned with gold bracelets and bands, brightened the room. After Margerie said hello, Barkov cut to the chase.

"You sit there." Pointing to a chair the consultation began. "Why are you here?"

Beginning a tale of broken dreams and financial woe Margerie rambled on. She paused several times and looked at the seer for direction, but none was given. When she wound down Malvina wrote something in a notebook. "Be still" she ordered, then closed her eyes.

After fifteen silent minutes Margerie said. "I hope I didn't blather on, but I can't seem to isolate what's wrong. Nothing moves Madam Barkov. Nothing changes."

Leaning back in her chair the great intuitive spoke. "You're wrong, there is movement always. Everything you talk about moves. Your whole story is motion, even talk about spiraling down." Lighting a Gauloise she savored the smoke before exhaling into an airless room. "Americans are spoiled, nothing is ever enough. You talk about things you don't have, won't adjust, just complain and get defensive." Radically she shifted gear. "You having sex with anyone?"

Startled, Margerie managed an answer. "Not now. It's been a while."

"Just as well. Big trouble at your age. You're too emotional. Emotions complicate things, create turmoil. Best you stay alone."

And Barkov charged on. "I see clouds floating in and out. You act to be appreciated, noticed. When work ends you get depressed. Women like you do not find work so depression builds. Unrecognized you feel stuck because you are stuck. How old are you?"

Stunned, she delivered her usual answer. "I don't believe in age."

Malvina shrugged her shoulders. "So don't believe. Age doesn't care. People know anyway. I know."

Feeling battered and blitzed, Margerie squirmed in her chair. Blessedly an assistant knocked on the door; another appointment was waiting. As unsettling as the session had been she was determined to remain civil. But studying her from behind a desk, the blunt clairvoyant had another psychic bulletin. "Wait, sit still. I see more. Your problem is clear, you seek to escape… hide, refuse to face things." Malvina paused before her final revelation. "And you drink too much."

Beneath heavy eyebrows the somber mystic watched Margerie get up. Back on her feet the frazzled truth seeker gathered her wits. Standing erect and glaring at Barkov she delivered a summation of her own. "You, Madam Birdbrain, are a windbag!" That said, she did a flawless turn and left in a theatrical huff.

58

Victor

Twenty-two and from the Midwest, Victor searched for where he belonged. He found it when he entered Manhattan. The New York press bemoaned pollution and crime but behind doom and gloom, change and vigor swept through the streets. Interest in politics, protest, and social responsibility diminished; a sexual revolution was in full swing. In spite of graffiti, rats, pollution, and muggings, innovation and liberation blossomed. The city struggled economically but low rents and open minds attracted creative outsiders. Unpredictable and accessible, Manhattan was worn down but red-hot.

Victor found a cheap loft on Broadway and 25th Street; an area teeming by day but deserted at night. At the Madison, one of few bars in the area, he sat next to an older woman paging through *Playbill*. After commenting on the weather, she asked where he was from. They talked about Chicago, their obscure Manhattan neighborhood, and the marvelous play she'd seen. Then Margerie Summers introduced herself.

The next day he saw her at a newsstand. "Why, hello there!" she said, then introduced him to her friend Elaine. "This is Victor Evans, our new neighbor from Chicago." Reaching out he shook her hand. "We're running late dear, but this was a delight. Serendipity!" Waving goodbye she and Elaine hurried down to the subway.

A week later he saw her again at the bar. She was hard to miss. A seasoned actress with short, bleached hair, her eyelids were shadowed aqua blue - a perfect acccent for fluttering, artificial eyelashes. Her cheerful voice passed through glossy red lips with an abundance of dears and darlings. And she always had something nice to say. "Well, here we are again Victor! Elaine thought you were so handsome you had to be an actor."

No matter where you were or what time it was there was something festive about her. Acting, design, theater, and film, even metaphysics and vitamins prompted a conversation. If the topic was creative or lifted the spirit, she was interested. Margerie knew priests, countermen, cab drivers, and tycoons; all of them by their first name. She'd listen to anyone down on their luck and conversed as easily with a tired hooker as a Long Island matron. Her outgoing nature attracted interesting people and if Vic was around he met them.

Like many big personalities, Margerie liked to drink and chatter. Her position on theater, film, or whatever seemed appropriate was delivered so well it was hard separating fact from fiction. Proudly claiming movie star Katie Summers as her doting niece, she'd tell anyone who'd listen what inside stuff was happening in Hollywood. Bill, the seen-it-all bartender at the Madison, said, "Half of what she says is shit." But Victor didn't care. If he was around when her speech slurred or she began to teeter, he'd take an arm and help her lesser-self stagger back to the Dorsey.

59

Arthur

Matriarch of a filthy rich family in Mississippi, Donna Lee Pruitt taught her children good manners, good taste, and how to savage a fool with a beguiling drawl. But the formidable southern belle could not control what she found Arthur doing with another boy in the garage.

Determined to restructure his manhood, she marched him off to the best military school in Dixie. But the rich loam of Mississippi had already produced an exotic bloom. When Arthur moved east Donna Lee feigned distress over losing a son to the Yankees; privately she sighed with relief.

Arthur's Manhattan life began in a Park Avenue duplex with Aunt Pearl, the sister his mother called "the naughty one." Divorced from husband number three, Pearl had lots of time to show her nephew the pleasures of New York. Young, blonde, and attractive, Arthur met men who found him, his body, and impudence, appealing. When advances were made, he kindly obliged and fell into bed with the best of them.

Wild about Tennessee Williams, Arthur was in the second row opening night for The Actor's Studio production, *Streetcar Named Desire*. Deeply moved by Margerie's portrayal of Blanche Dubois, he waited by the stage door to congratulate her. The next day he sent a dozen roses. Over the years they ran into each other in bars, at parties, or on the street. Drawn to her theatrical passion he became a loyal friend. As far as Arthur was concerned, she'd always be special; he'd seen her play Blanche in '52.

60

Ask him

A savvy usher, Margerie knew how to sneak
someone into a Broadway show. Nearing the end of
a long run she got Victor into a seat for *Sleuth*.
Afterwards they went to Joe Allen's for a nightcap.
Sitting alone at the bar, Arthur Pruitt saw her and
waved them over. Southern cordial, he bought the
drinks and his acid wit kept them laughing until last
call.

Cabbing back to their neighborhood Victor
mentioned how attractive Arthur was. A bit tipsy,
Margerie said he was sixty-two and flew to London
every year for plastic surgery, then shared her own
secret for eternal youth; Vitamin C.

If he was prowling through the gay bars, Vic
frequently ran into Arthur. Aways holding court, his
fluctuating entourage called him "Corby," and

Corby bought drinks for anyone who looked interesting. Discreetly turning aside, he'd confide in Victor and share his assessments. "See that blonde? He's dumb as a stump but has an ass like two honeydew melons." After scathing reviews Arthur would turn and face his fans with a duplicitous smile. Even when vicious he sounded polite.

Arthur invited Margerie and Vic to a housewarming at Johnny Rockwell's lavish apartment and insisted they wear something smart. Arriving late they grabbed a drink and found Arthur sitting with a group of attractive young men. One of them, a hairdresser from Queens, was showing off a boyfriend who worked for Lagerfeld in Paris. After fielding questions about the legendary designer, he pretentiously translated English into French for his current lover.

Arthur had been in Paris a dozen times but never learned the language. Margerie could tell he found the translating parvenu annoying. When the moderator addressed the man known by a different name, all heads turned towards the genteel aristocrat. "Corby, there must be something you'd like to know. Trust me, Bernard knows absolutely everything about Lagerfeld."

The southern gentleman took a sip of scotch then answered the puffed-up pretender. "Ask him" Arthur said in a genteel drawl, "how big his dick is."

61

Verification

Margerie met Ron Hartfeld in 1953. A young talent manager who had taken a chance, he moved to L.A., and became a successful talent agent. In town on business, she invited Victor to join them for drinks at Charlie's.

Hollywood producers had a passion for New York talent. Luring actors to the West Coast with contracts and money made Hartfeld rich, but he admitted the magic of performance was in theater, not on film. Reminiscing, they talked about who made it, who did not, and loyalists that would never abandon Broadway.

After excusing herself for the powder room, Vic asked Ron about two of Margerie's claims: Katie Summers and triumph at The Actor's Studio. Ron confirmed the Hollywood star was indeed her niece, but an early divorce interrupted the extent of their relationship. And yes, he'd seen her performance in *Streetcar Named Desire*. Lots of people, himself included, expected her to have a successful career; sadly, nothing happened. Lifting his glass, he made a sardonic toast to the cruel world of theater and Broadway politics.

Margerie started back. The restaurant lighting was soft and flattering, she looked radiant, poised, and self-assured. Gliding gracefully between tables she dipped down here and there to say hello, then tilting her head, smiled and waved at someone before moving on. In spite of everything, they both knew she still could capture a room.

62

Showtime

A chorus girl at the Copacabana and girlfriend of gangster Tony Fabrazzi, Bernice Stratton disappeared for two decades, then returned to run the Copa coat check. Anyone nostalgic for the nightclub's heyday was interested in her story. Bernice got a lot of publicity.

Busty and beautiful, she lived in a two-room suite at the Dorsey Hotel and met Margerie on the elevator. Sharing a table in the coffee shop they somehow discovered they were born on the same day: December 4th, 1915. "Promise me now" Bernice teased, "we won't tell a soul while we're still lookin' good!"

Two years later Bernice left the Copa, did some promotions, and was putting together a cabaret act. Whenever she saw Margerie she'd flash a showgirl smile and say, "Hey girl, still lookin' good!"

Coming home from a Wednesday matinee, Margerie noticed an ambulance in front of the hotel. By the time she reached the building two attendants were carrying out a covered body. Rushing in, she went to the front desk.

"Frank. My God, what happened?"

"Brace yourself," the desk clerk said grimly, "It's Bernice Stratton. She called from her room for help and those medics got here fast, like in ten minutes. But they were too late... she was gone." Frank lowered his voice and stared at her. "I wasn't surprised you know, I sensed it coming. That's how it happens." He snapped a finger in front of her face. "Just like that." Leaning closer, he repeated it. "Just like that!" Staring at her, he snapped his finger again.

Margerie couldn't sleep. In three weeks they both would've turned sixty. Two days earlier Bernice showed her a headshot for the cabaret act, made her promise to be there opening night. She looked happy, energized, could pass for 40... still lookin' good.

Along with the terrible news, what happened at the front desk bothered her. Frank had been at the Dorsey for years; Elaine thought he was creepy. Over and over he told Margerie he was psychic, could foresee death and had special gifts. She thought he was odd and left it at that. Now she was upset. What made him act that way, emphasize "just like that" then focus on her? Why did he zero in, stare, then snap a finger? And he did it twice... like a warning.

Her heart was racing, she started to sweat. When panic set in Margerie tried reasoning it out. The city abounded with frauds claiming to be clairvoyant and Malvina Barkov was a prime example. Been there, done that, she told herself: you learned a lesson, now let it go. After breathing deeply and repeating all-is-well she began calming down.

Honoring Bernice with white roses would be a nice gesture she thought. Tomorrow I'll get a paper and check the obituaries, see if a funeral is planned. Maybe I'll call the cabaret, get information from them.... someone will know. One thing Margerie knew for sure; she wouldn't ask Frank.

63

Mistaken identity

Applying for an Actor's Equity card in 1953, Margerie discovered another actress had registered the same name. She dealt with the problem by adding 'et' to her last name and after that was professionally labeled Margerie Summerset. The other Marjorie Summers, five years younger, appeared in several Broadway hits then moved to Hollywood. After appearing in four films, she faded from view.

Margerie's theatrical savvy dazzled out-of-towners who wandered into the Madison Bar. When someone asked for her name she gave the one she'd been given at birth. If they said they'd heard of her she'd smile, take a sip of her drink, and change the subject. If they remembered a play or film starring the same-name actress she'd head for the ladies room. More often than not, mistaken identity boosted her mystique.

In May of 1975, a brief obituary in the New York Times said notable actress Marjorie Summers, 55, had moved on. A week later the same name was having her second drink in the Madison when Joe McPherson walked in. New in town, he'd spent several nights chatting with her. Now he stood there in shock.

"Good Lord," he gasped, "I thought you were dead!"

Trying her best, she feigned concern. "Oh my, what a muddle! People did get us confused. You see my stage name isn't Summers… I put a tiny 'e-t' at the end because of Actor's Equity. It's Summerset dear." Coquettishly tilting her head she smiled then redeemed herself. "Now really Joe, did you think I was that old?"

64

Tuesday in June

After a restful night of sleep Margerie got out of
bed, looked outside, and smiled at the world. There
were no aches, no worries, the sun was shining, and
she could spend a Tuesday in June however she
wanted.

Walking to Times Square she passed the Broadway
marquees with gratitude, was thankful for living at
the apex of American theater. Checking a work
schedule at the Shubert, the General Manager
passed by: tapped her shoulder, smiled, and told her
to have a good day. A cloudless blue sky crowned
the city. It was a balmy seventy-four; people slowed
down, and everyone looked pleased. She picked up
Variety, got a popsicle, lipstick, and a pair of
nylons, then caught a train going back downtown.

The subway car was empty except for a young Black man sitting across from her. Wearing a white sleeveless t-shirt, his muscled arms held a baby who reached out from across the aisle. When Margerie smiled the baby laughed, so the father got up, came over, and sat beside her. "He wants to meet you," he said proudly. "This is my son Luther." Leaning in a tiny hand touched her face, then he looked at his father and laughed again. Getting off at the next stop they turned around and waved. "Goodbye little Luther," she called out before the door closed, "goodbye Dad." The train moved on.

Back on 28th street there was no reason to hurry home so she walked to Madison Square. Sitting on a secluded bench she thought about Luther's father, how his strong arms cradled and protected his son. When a red bird flew over and perched at the end of the bench, she didn't move. Slowly the tiny creature hopped closer, looked up and began to chirp. Then something happened, something instantaneous and overwhelming. Ecstasy surged through her whole being. The sensation was so intense it obliterated sound, vision, and any sense of being in a particular place. Snatched from everything familiar, Margerie was suspended in a conscious state of total bliss.

It was 3:30 when she sat down; now, glancing at the clock towering over the park, it was ten after five. The bird had left, people going home scurried through the park, traffic noise and density returned. She stared at her hands then cleared her throat.

Margerie chose not to tell anyone. On a Tuesday in June, sitting in a park, she entered a different state of being. Yearning to repeat the experience, she hoped rapture would return. Suspended in a place without logic, fear, or control, was impossible to describe. Hoping to be taken again, to languish in bliss, wasn't enough; she prayed what happened would capture the world.

65

Everybody

Margerie met him first and felt responsible. Sitting next to her in the Madison, Jean Luc shared his story of working on a freighter to reach New York. The handsome young Frenchman hoped to find work as a chef. Eager to help, she introduced him to anyone who might have a lead.

When Gina Cerbone strolled in on a Wednesday night, she signaled her over. Raised in a mob-connected family, the flamboyant Sicilian had a raw sense of humor and was candidly open. Once she pulled a silver gun from her purse and told Margerie, "It keeps the creeps away." Gina bought drinks, teased Jean Luc about his English, and brazenly flirted until last call. Saying goodnight on the street, she was a bit surprised to see them walk off holding hands.

On Saturday night Margerie came in late. Victor was talking with Jean Luc at the other end of the bar but by the time she got a drink they'd left. A few days later Vic called to say his new friend was having a tough time so moved in with him.

After getting a nasty cold, Elaine lectured her friend about late night drinking. To keep the peace Margerie suspended socializing. On the way home from work she looked across the street and saw Jean Luc stumbling up the steps of the Prince George Hotel. He was with an older, inebriated woman.

She ventured back into the Madison a month later and was enjoying a glass of chardonnay when Gina roared through the door. Taking a stool she slammed her purse on the bar and cut to the chase. "Have you seen that parlez-vous fucker? I swear on my grandmother's grave if he walks through the door I'll blow his balls off!"

For a moment Margerie was speechless. "Gina. What on earth is going on?"

"Trust me, you don't want to know. If you see him or his buddy Victor tell 'em to watch out! I'm outta here." Gina grabbed her bag and stomped into the night.

The next day she got an agitated call from Vic. Jean Luc had disappeared. He took $60, a radio, his leather jacket, and left him with a dose of clap.

Having breakfast with Elaine in the hotel coffee shop, they split the Sunday Times. Drawn to sordid news on the front-page, Margerie saw that a former governor, seventy-four, had a heart attack during intercourse with a twenty-three-year-old intern. Rushed from the Waldorf Astoria to the emergency room, he was dead on arrival. His wife, affectionately called Cookie, was in Boca Raton visiting grandchildren. Services were pending.

Finishing a triangle of toast, Margerie put the paper down. "My God, you need a sexual scorecard." she said to no one in particular. "Everyone's doing everybody."

66

Last call

Loneliness meant late nights at the Madison. It was after eleven when she took a seat at the bar by an attractive man. A recent transplant from Los Angeles, Dan insisted on buying the drinks. Their conversation evolved into an unexpected, playful flirtation.

After disclosing his affair with a mature movie star, the forty-four-year-old extolled involvements with older women. On his third vodka stinger, he reached under the bar and put a hand on Margerie's knee. Taken by surprise, she snapped "Watch it boy," then turned on the barstool and crossed her legs. "New York women can't be had for a couple of drinks" she said, but instead of sounding urbane, her voice quivered and lost its impact.

"Calm down sweetheart, the world's still spinning," Dan teased. "I misread the signals." Grinning, he stood up. "Time to stroll around." That said, he headed for the other end of the bar.

Perturbed but flattered, she pulled a five-dollar bill from her bra and ordered another drink. Her admirer was joking with a brassy blonde laughing at something he said. Annoyed, Margerie let other issues surface. Her bathroom sink was clogged, a back tooth felt sensitive, and on her way-out Ray Ginetti said she looked "puffy." No man had shown interest in her since Segundo.

Dan looked pleased with his younger prospect. Tilting back on her stool, she sucked on a straw suggestively as he whispered in her ear. Hoping she would tip over, Margerie had an idea. Getting up she walked towards the ladies room, unclasped her purse, then discreetly turned it upside down. Everything inside fell on the floor.

"Oh my," she cried, "look what I've done! Stuff all over the place." The only one who seemed to notice was an elderly man who crouched down to gather what he could. Stuffing things back into her purse she said, "You're a dear. This silly bag popped itself open out of nowhere."

When the bartender announced last call, the lights in the Madison went on. It was almost 2 am. After loud good-byes to the bartender, she waved at the California hustler but wasn't sure he noticed. Outside on deserted Twenty-Eighth Street, freezing rain bounced around as it hit the pavement. Bracing herself, Margerie wearily pulled her black coat in close then started walking back to the Dorsey. She stopped twice, turned around and looked, but no one was following.

67

Heat wave

August of '79 was hot as hell. After cooling off at an afternoon movie, Margerie stopped at Belmore Cafeteria for iced tea and a salad. Picking up a discarded paper she saw the gruesome headline:

BROADWAY DANCER STABBED IN
MADISON SQUARE!

The photo of a chalk outline surrounding a bloody stain took up half a page. A twenty-two-year-old man, who'd danced in *CATS*, had been stabbed to death sometime after midnight.

Three blocks from the Dorsey Hotel, Madison Square was a neighborhood refuge. Opinions varied on what happened. Not surprised, Elaine said the city was full of maniacs. Coffee shop owner Gus Papadakis thought the murder had something to do with drugs. Rose believed an innocent young man was just escaping the heat, in the wrong place at the wrong time. But Margerie knew what happened after dark in Madison Square; gay men cruised for pick-ups. Justifying his own action in the park, Ray Ginetti claimed convenience came with the territory. "Why drag someone home if you can take care of business behind a tree?"

It bothered her. For decades she'd heard about robberies, beatings, and worse from gay men. She implored Victor to be on guard, but when he said not to worry felt he was brushing her off. During dinner with Elaine she voiced her concern. "I just don't get it," Margerie said. "All these wonderful men. It's got to be more than sex. What do they need… why do they take so many risks?"

THE 1980S

68

Glasses

Accustomed to getting compliments on her eyes, a director said they were "cerulean blue, like the Aegean Sea." But when the head usher saw Margerie leading people to the wrong seats, her cherished attribute yielded to optics.

Even though tickets, small print, and performers on stage came into focus, she vowed never to wear glasses except at work. Slowly relaxing the rule, she occasionally allowed vanity and vision to coexist.

A few years later things got blurry again. When an optometrist suggested bifocals, she recoiled in horror. The very thought of granny-glasses induced a panic attack. Margerie found a solution at Woolworth's. Plastic Japanese eyewear cost a dollar, so she got three pairs of varied strengths and kept them in her purse. Determined to keep obstructions off her face, they served their purpose only when necessary.

Nearing the end of a long run, she had no problem sneaking an elocution student into *Jesus Christ Superstar*. After the curtain rose, she met Randy in the lobby and took him to an empty seat. Later they walked to Joe Allen's for a drink.

One drink led to another. After putting on glasses to read small print in a *Stagebill* bio, it suddenly got quiet. All heads turned as famous actor David Payson entered the room. Placing her glasses on the bar she reached out to grab him before he passed by.

"David, how marvelous to see you!" Clutching his arm, she continued. "I want you to meet Randy Dell, a student of mine ready to roll after rave reviews in Kansas City." Unable to place her he shook the young actor's hand, chatted a bit, then joined friends waiting at a table. Knowing the whole room had witnessed the encounter, Margerie basked in the light of associative recognition.

It was getting late. Randy suggested they share a cab going downtown. Still reveling in her interaction with a major star, Margerie began a poised departure.

Her exit was unexpectedly interrupted. "Hey lady," yelled the bartender.

Turning, she faced him with measured reserve. "Yes?"

He'd left his station and was coming towards her with something in his hand. Sneaking a look at David Payson she knew he was watching.

Holding out a pair of cheap pink spectacles the bartender said, "I think you left these on the bar."

After a glance she looked him straight in the eye. "Sorry dear, wrong person. Those aren't mine." Then Margerie made it perfectly clear. "I don't wear glasses."

That said, with head held high, she did a perfect turn and majestically left the room.

69

Count

Her friend Rose worried about her niece. A six-foot tall high school senior, Richelle Schmidt was shy and insecure; a sad soul trapped in the body of an NBA player. Her concerned parents owned a thriving butcher shop in Queens and would do anything to help their daughter. When Rose recommended Margerie Summers as a transformational coach, they eagerly signed on.

Using an Actor's Equity card, Margerie reserved a small studio in Town Hall and their sessions began. Suffering under a crown of thick curly hair inherited from her Bulgarian grandmother, Richelle's low self-esteem hid beneath a sweet disposition. Focusing on simple things, her coach told her she had flawless skin, expressive brown eyes, and an inviting smile. Comparing those features to models in magazines broadened her pupil's perspective.

They talked about fashion, etiquette, beauty, and boys. Richelle said towering over classmates felt awkward, that large hands and feet were embarrassing. Even so, she was captain of the tennis team and most of the kids liked her. Margerie noticed a splendid figure hiding beneath a poorly chosen wardrobe and was delighted with her sense of humor. Working on posture and positive thinking, she emphasized height was empowering and demanded attention. Declaring change as the elixir of life, the teacher encouraged her student to re-invent herself.

Recently retired, Madge Biddle was a Broadway stylist who occasionally saw clients in her apartment. After Coach Summers explained the Cinderella project her friend agreed to help. Leaping into the unknown wasn't easy for the tall girl from Queens, but when she found out that Madge had worked on Elizabeth Taylor and Jane Fonda, Richelle gave in. A week later they took a subway to the Upper West Side for a Biddle makeover.

Anxiously awaiting the results, Margerie drank coffee and paged through magazines. When her protege appeared four hours later the transformation left her speechless.

After relaxing thick curly hair, Madge gave Richelle a short Italian cut that emphasized a long neck and perfect cheekbones. Shaping eyebrows and curling lashes made her big brown eyes look inviting and sensual. To finish the look, she'd applied a neutral foundation, matte finish, and pink lipstick. Biddle's professional makeover turned an awkward girl into a stunning woman.

Back on the street heads turned. When a construction worker on West 72nd whistled, Richelle blushed and said, "I can't believe it."

"Yes you can! Believe it," her teacher told her. "Then embrace it."

Wardrobe came next. Combing through stores in Herald Square they bought skirts, sweaters, blouses, and shoes; even found a black strapless dress that showed off Richelle's considerable cleavage. Back in Queens her parents were thrilled; the phone rang, and friends called. Then Dan Granger, six-foot-seven captain of the basketball team, asked her to the Senior Prom.

During their final session Richelle practiced walking in heels. When her coach learned getting to the dance floor meant walking down a flight of stairs, she taught her student how to make an entrance.

Employing a strategy used by Hollywood bombshell Lana Turner, Margerie began instruction in front of a mirror. "Honor the power of an entrance," she told her. "Before walking into a room or coming downstairs, stop. Stand still and let them see you; Richelle Schmidt has arrived!" Her impassioned coach continued "Breathe into the diaphragm then count. Not too fast, one…two…that's it. Now turn your head, look side to side. Three…four…look around, survey your territory. Exhale." She continued. "Easy now…five and six, seven…eight. You've got their attention so smile, they're watching." Hard to believe anyone could miss her, Richelle did as she was told. "You're beautiful, own it! Take Dan's arm, we're at nine then ten…now begin your descent."

Proudly looking at her protege, Margerie summarized the technique used by a glamorous star. "Remember to always pause before you enter a room. Claim your presence, let them see you! And dear, don't forget to count!"

70

Paso Doble

After arriving in New York, it only took a week for Elaine to find a job. Joining the secretarial pool for a consulting firm, she made herself available to stay late and work on weekends. Dedication paid off; a year later she was managing twelve typists. Direct and systematic, subordinates found Elaine humorless but agreed she could be counted on to get things done.

Passionate about clothes, she filled her closet with working-girl dresses and appropriate shoes. She liked the theater and occasionally saw a movie but was content reading a novel or combing through marked-down racks at Macy's. Encouraging her to be more interactive, Margerie suggested she take ballroom dancing lessons at Arthur Murray's. It turned out to be a perfect fit. Quickly advancing from the basics, she began private lessons with a handsome instructor from Buenos Aires. The first man to put a hand on the small of her back, Reynaldo Santiago knew how to control a step and rein her in.

After every lesson another woman waited in reception for her own twirl with Reynaldo. A flamboyant Italian, Sylvie Ricci's ample breasts seemed right at home in plunging necklines she adorned with gold jewelry. Chatting while putting on her coat, Elaine learned Sylvie was divorced, lived in Freeport, and had been taking lessons for five months. Once she called Santiago 'Senor Hot' and two weeks later referred to him as her 'devil doll.'

Elaine felt surprisingly competitive and began strategically preparing for Tuesday nights. Margerie helped with make-up and what to wear then spritzed her with Shalimar before she left. Gloriously spinning around a private room with Reynaldo sustained her for the week. Even her strictly-business boss noticed a change. "Miss Reilly," he said one morning, "you look radiant today."

The first of March was damp and ugly. Stalled on the subway she was an hour late for work; at the office three typists called in sick. At quarter past six she rushed home, got dressed, then raced back to mid-town. Hurrying to the studio in heavy rain she arrived two minutes before a scheduled lesson.

When the door to Studio B opened, a short, barrel-chested man greeted her. Armand told her he was a substituting for Mr. Santiago and that they'd be doing the cha-cha-cha. Enamored as he was with his own twists and turns, Elaine feared Armand's toupee would fly off at any moment but somehow got through a gruesome hour. On her way out she was surprised not to see Sylvie.

The following week she called to confirm her lesson with Reynaldo and was told he was unavailable. Asking if he was well, the receptionist said, "Oh yes, Mr. Santiago is fine. He's moved to Freeport and at some point, will resume work on Long Island."

Back at the hotel she waited for Margerie to come home then went to her room. "What is it with women like that?" she sobbed. "The flashy ones with their claws out always get the good men."

Knowing it was Elaine's first romantic meltdown, Margerie tried to be comforting. "I know how upsetting this is, but don't worry. If Reynaldo is anything like you say he'll be back." And with a New Yorker's logic explained why. "Trust me dear, I guarantee it. Nothing happens in Freeport."

71

Calling Dr. Chang

Margerie's legs symbolized her struggle; for years she had trouble moving forward. Month after month walking got harder. The day she turned sixty-five Elaine gave her a blouse and an aluminum cane along with advice to tell anyone that asked she'd sprained her ankle. The next day feeling down and decrepit, Margerie fortuitously ran into a dancer she knew. Alarmed at her condition, he suggested an acupuncturist in Chinatown who had worked wonders on his sciatic nerve. She had nothing to lose so went back to her room and called. A polite young voice, Dr. Chang's granddaughter, answered the phone then scheduled an appointment.

His office was above a dim sum restaurant on Pell Street. Climbing a flight of stairs, she entered a small reception area where jasmine incense hid any trace of the cooking below. A white cat brushed up against her leg then a door opened; Dr. Chang gestured for her to come into his treatment room.

After locating the pain, he assembled tools of the trade. Before piercing, he smiled and said, "No pain, just pinches," then strategically inserted thin needles into her legs and ankles. When that was done, he took a hand and checked her pulse.

The following day she took off for work without the cane and confidently ushered people to their seats. She had two sessions with Dr. Chang and the results were amazing. Deeply grateful, she urged anyone experiencing pain to see the miraculous healer in Chinatown.

72

Cab fare

When the economy took off, low-cost housing disappeared. Welfare recipients, the homeless, and mentally challenged, flooded streets that looked like Calcutta. After a public outcry the city paid exorbitant fees for whatever housing they could find. Taking advantage of the situation, investors scooped up residential hotels and took the city for all they could. Long-term tenants had two options: deal with it or move.

When a foreign consortium bought the Dorsey Hotel, they replaced the staff with a crew that could barely speak English. After cutting security they discontinued housekeeping; towels or sheets could be picked up at the front desk on the first of the month. Boom-boxes, dirty elevators, and hallways reeking of marijuana and Jiffy Pop were bad enough, but it was the broken switchboard and no heat that exasperated Margerie. A belligerent mother with two screaming kids moved into the room next to Elaine's; even with earplugs she couldn't sleep. Fed up, they stormed the front desk together.

Munching on banana chips the manager ignored them. "Mr. Quasaab, I've lived here for twenty years," Margerie said. "Miss Reilly's been here for ten. The hallways are filthy, the heat's off, and there's no security. Non-residents roam around day and night. We don't feel safe, can't sleep, and nobody does anything."

Licking salty fingers he exposed his tea-stained teeth. "So?" he snickered.

Margerie's was outraged "Excuse me, did you just say that? So? If you don't do something we'll call the Health Department, mayor's office, and the police." Shrugging his shoulders he looked away and turned on a radio.

"Did you hear me? Act like a manager and do your job!" she demanded. "If this continues we're both moving out."

Unmoved he faced them. "Go on, do it. And do it soon. I'll pay for the cab."

73

So Convenient

Retirees, singles, artists, and those with a limited income, had trouble finding housing in Manhattan. Displaced hordes moved to Queens, Brooklyn, and points beyond. Fed up, Ray Ginetti put his bags in a cab, told the driver to wait, then smashed a dozen eggs on the Dorsey's front desk. After giving management the finger, he spit on the floor and headed for Hoboken.

An accountant at work told Elaine about a residential hotel on East 53rd. She said it was reasonably priced, well managed, and that tenants were screened. Elaine made an appointment for the following day.

A seven-story building on a prosperous block, the Hewitt Hotel was owned by the family that built it in 1934. Dated but respectable, the genteel lobby had a man in a suit and tie behind the front desk. The manager described tenants as professionals who liked the location. Scanning their applications, she was satisfied with Elaine's position at a reliable firm but looked dubiously at the other applicant's vocational claim: Drama Coach. Stressing the Hewitt was residential and did not allow professional visits, Margerie claimed she had a private studio then changed the subject.

"The Hewitt will be so convenient when my niece visits," she said, then name-dropped Katie Summers. "Katie always stays at the Plaza and I'll only be ten blocks away!" The reference worked and Margerie avoided divulging an income that came from seating people.

A sparsely furnished apartment with two tiny bedrooms, a center room, Pullman kitchen and bath, was available on the fifth floor in ten days. It was small and cost more than their rooms on 28th street but they were determined to make it happen. Elaine promised she'd walk to work, Margerie agreed to cut back on eating out. Cheerfully they signed a two-year lease and let The Dorsey deteriorate without them.

74

Too good to be true

The rooms were small and space was limited but compromising was worth it. Margerie had new territory to explore, and Elaine joyfully walked eight blocks to work instead of taking the crowded subway.

It felt like a different city. Streets were clean, it was quiet, and people dressed well. Their upscale neighborhood had an abundance of markets, boutiques, cafes, and restaurants. They saw Katherine Hepburn strolling down 53rd street and were sure the woman under a crumpled hat in D'Agostino's was legendary film star Greta Garbo. Proud to claim the Hewitt as their new address, Elaine said it was too good to be true; a sentiment that crystallized during their third month of bliss.

Margerie saw it first, an envelope with the Hewitt logo slipped under their door. A single page got right to the point. The frayed but reputable hotel had been sold to New York's largest developer, Kaldikoff Enterprises. The new owner was converting the building into luxury condominiums; regretting any inconvenience, tenants had 60 days to vacate.

75

Conversion

It was the 1980's. Having, making, and faking wealth, became fashionable when Ronald Reagan moved into the White House. Flip and sarcastic replaced hip and fantastic. Being rich and discreet was old school boring; the nouveau riche was conspicuous and brash. Designer clothes, Rolex watches, and flashy jewels were de rigueur and so was flaunting it. The south Bronx, nonconformity, and self-discovery were yesterday's news. It was time to make a killing, re-invest, and spend more.

After a decade of decline, real estate was the hottest game in town. Throughout Manhattan rental apartments were converted into co-ops or condos. Renovated brownstones in "iffy" areas got sold to the highest bidders. Rent controls vanished, stabilizations disappeared, and poor neighborhoods "gentrified." Anyone who couldn't afford to buy space found themselves in a housing desert.

New owners of the Hewitt, Kaldikoff Enterprises dropped all protocols. Stripping the lobby of rugs and furniture, they ignored burned out bulbs, let the floors get dirty, and replaced the polite man at the front desk with a disheveled security guard. Every question got the same response: call management. If you did no one answered.

Activists protested to save their neighborhoods, but conversions snowballed. In the meantime, developers offered settlements to get unwilling tenants out; if that didn't work, they made life unbearable. Stunned like two deer in headlight, Margerie and Elaine had no idea where to go or how to get there.

76

Expect the Good

When demolition started, dust and debris joined intolerable racket. Every day was irritating; no one answered questions because no one cared. Life at the Hewitt turned into chaos. Margerie's spirit needed fortifying.

She'd read his books and believed in the teaching but needed personal help. A busy man, Dr. Parker's fee for a consultation was expensive. She skipped lunches, saved change, borrowed the rest, then made an appointment.

In a mahogany paneled office, Dr. Parker greeted her from behind a Regency desk. After she sat down, he began with a question. "How can I help?" Margerie explained her stressful situation. Familiar with the Hewitt and conversions, he'd heard about unsavory methods used to empty a building. He also knew large settlements were paid to get people out. Zeroing in on her what-can-I-do muddle, he urged Margerie to realign and have faith in a perfect resolution.

"Stop focusing on the worst and expect the good," he told her. "Let the Power that created you handle it. You've locked the door now open it up." Nurturing but direct, he continued his counsel. "You know the teaching and you've read the books so it's up to you. Refute negative thinking! Write the truth on a piece of paper then read it, repeat it, and say it out loud: I Witness God As Miracles! Period." It was the synoptic blast she needed. He gave her a business card with another directive. "This is my private number. When the calamity ends call and leave a message on my machine. Just say Dr. Parker, you were right." The session was over.

For two months she'd been on a list at Legal Aid; the next day she got a call. A Brooklyn lawyer, Gabriel Birnbaum, was eager to bring corporate mercenaries to their knees. For 25% of a settlement, he'd lead the unfortunates out of purgatory.

Courageously they soldiered on. Elaine called Gabe their guardian angel; he was there each step of the way. Every night before sleeping Margerie visualized making a call, holding the phone, and leaving a message: "Dr. Parker, you were right."

77

Alarming news

Margerie heard about it first from Victor. A brief article buried in back of the paper, said 19 young men in New York had died from a mysterious virus. The victims were gay so no one paid much attention.

By 1985 fatalities were soaring:1400 men in the city had died and it was getting worse. AIDS was on track to become a global nightmare. Poorly equipped hospitals and drugs that did not deliver created rampant anxiety in what used to be a carefree gay world. Margerie encouraged Victor to meditate, lay low and be careful. Politicians and the public weren't as interested. Homosexual men were promiscuous; it was their problem.

Two unlikely people stepped forward. Taking a break from her sixth marriage, movie star Elizabeth

Taylor jumped into the muck. Demanding action, she raised a million dollars for medical research. Mother Teresa, a compassionate activist, also refused to ignore the spiraling horror. She flew in from Calcutta with a team of nuns and opened an AIDS hospice in Greenwich Village.

Being gay wasn't fun anymore. Vic worried about symptoms, incubation, and vulnerable friends. In spite of the diligence and passion he had poured into a fashion project, it collapsed. His confidence fell with it. Worn out, working two jobs and barely functioning, he received a knockout blow from his landlord; they were converting his building into condominiums. Over a cup of tea, he told Margerie everything was screwed up and it was time to go. After 17 years in paradise, Victor left Manhattan for parts unknown.

78

Go girl

Five months passed and nine remaining tenants got their fifth final notice. Kaldikoff Enterprises offered $25,000 and three weeks to vacate; if they didn't accept, construction would commence anyway. Exasperated and fatigued, everyone settled except two determined women: Margerie and Elaine.

A month later every wall on the fifth floor except theirs had been torn down; their apartment looked like a single box in an empty warehouse. Interior demolition went as far as it could but no one budged. Fed up with being pushed around they toughened up. When two burly goons knocked on their door with an ultimatum, Elaine yelled "fuck off" and slammed the door. After that, things got worse. The elevator didn't work, hot water stopped, and garbage piled up. Demanding basic service Gabe filed counterclaims, writs, and made calls to Kaldikoff they ignored.

On a November night after climbing up five flights for the fourth time that week they opened their door. Turning on the light they watched a dozen mice scamper across the floor. Screaming hysterically Elaine raced down the steps into the street; Margerie trailed behind her. When they called Gabe from a pay phone he was prepared. Shrewd and dependable, he played his trump card.

In half an hour a news team from Channel 7 stormed past security and hiked up dimly lit steps to the fifth floor. Margerie was magnificent. Fully made up and wearing a red turban, she dramatically pointed out the broken elevator, burned out lights, and turned a waterless faucet on and off. After that, she led the cameras into the bathroom where four mice cowered in a corner. In the meantime, Elaine sobbed on the couch for an investigative reporter. Red-hot television, the riveting exposé ran that night at nine, eleven, and throughout the following day.

The next morning the Daily News and New York Post sent photographers over. Strangers offered encouragement, people standing outside gazed towards the 5th floor. A black transvestite in thigh-high boots recognized Margerie on Lexington Avenue, lit up and yelled, "You go girl!"

On Friday night when Elaine got home from work, a man in a gray suit was waiting with Margerie in the dismantled lobby. Representing Kaldikoff, he'd gotten them rooms in the New York Hilton and was sending a car on Monday so they could meet with the owner. When Elaine mentioned bringing Gabe, the suit balked, but after they walked away agreed to terms.

With PhD's in Victimology, Margerie, Elaine, and Gabriel Birnbaum walked into the oppressor's office to conclude a deal. The indomitable twosome received $150,000 in a joint, tax-free settlement along with 60 days housing in a mid-range hotel. Gabe got a separate $35,000 fee. After agreeing to non-disclosure, the trio gathered their papers. Then with checks in hand, left Kaldikoff and combat behind them.

79

What they'd need

With only two weeks left in the hotel Kaldikoff paid for, they still hadn't found a place to live. Hoping to remain in an upscale neighborhood their search was fruitless.

Passing a building on East Fifty-Fourth, Margerie said hello to the doorman and on a whim, asked if he knew of any rentals. Surprisingly, he said a condo owner was renting an apartment on the lobby floor. She got the number, thanked him profusely, then hurried back to wait for Elaine. That night they called Abby Roth and made an appointment.

A wary widow, Mrs. Roth owned three apartments in the building. As she scrutinized the unusual twosome, Margerie sensed her reserve and raised their profile by mentioning her famous niece and claiming Elaine was personal attaché to big-shot John Debbing. After that Roth loosened up.

The apartment had a good-sized living room, bedroom with walk-in closets, a nice bath, small kitchen, and hardwood floors. But situated on the lobby floor it virtually got no light. Acknowledging the shortcoming, Roth said an identical unit on the fourth floor rented for $2000 instead of $1500 for the one they were in. Claiming to have another appointment Elaine agreed to call the following day.

A good deal, it still was a lot of money. Margerie could sleep in the living room so they'd need a convertible couch, a bed for Elaine, and appropriate furniture. There would also be telephone and utility bills to pay. Elaine needed those big closets for her clothes and wanted to stay in the area. Her roommate liked the convenience of a market across the street, a bookstore and deli around the corner. Anxious to experience better living and tired of furnished housing, they slowly upscaled. "Maybe it does cost more," Margerie rationalized, "but it is the East 50s." Then considering new circumstances, came up with another reason "And really dear, we do need a doorman." The next day they signed a two-year lease.

80

Lifeline

Months of turmoil had taken its toll; walking got hard again. After settling into the condo rental, Margerie's first priority was acupuncture treatment with the amazing Dr. Chang. Determined to sustain mobility, Margerie eagerly called her lifeline in Chinatown.

When his granddaughter answered the phone, she recognized her gentle voice and asked for an appointment. For a moment she paused then politely apologized. "I'm sorry, but my grandfather is in heaven."

THE 1990s

81

Excuse me

It was frustrating but she adjusted. Margerie could move around the apartment with a cane but venturing out required a wheelchair. Elaine got everything they needed in the neighborhood. If something required attention, like a clogged drain or burned-out bulb, building services took good care of them. Living in a service building was delightful.

If she was running errands on weekends, Elaine wheeled Margerie into the lobby so she could chat with Hector: her favorite doorman. After his daughter was born, they bought clothes for the baby and sent his wife a box of Godiva chocolates. Hector had the lowdown on those he served; like the bride in 7E cheating on her older husband or the teenage terror in 10A who got drunk every weekend. But the real gems were about the venom that poured through the lips of Marcy Korff.

Abby Roth said Mrs. Korff was so abominable that Moses would cross the Red Sea again just to avoid her. Scoring big on her third divorce, Marcy got five million and a three-bedroom penthouse on the top floor. One morning when Elaine ventured a cheery hello, Korff sneered, barged in front of her and rushed through the door.

On a Sunday afternoon Margerie was in the lobby when Marcy swept in. Glaring at the woman in the wheelchair she sneered, turned. and got into the elevator. Embarrassed, she asked Hector if her lipstick was askew or if something else was wrong. "Don't pay attention to that snake," he said, "she's toxic. Around here we call her Brobit, the Bronx Bitch." Hoping to soothe her feelings Hector pulled a brown paper bag out of his desk. "Hey, I forgot. These are for you. Brownies my wife baked."

Three weeks later, anxious to get to a sale, Elaine waited impatiently for her roommate to get it together. After putting on makeup and a strand of turquoise beads, Margerie wrapped an orange scarf around her head and got wheeled into the lobby.

Hector had a Celia Cruz CD waiting for her, so she put on his clunky headphones. Chewing gum and swaying to a tropical beat, the weather was about to change; Hurricane Marcy was on the way. When Korff appeared at the door she waited for Hector to open it then roared in and stopped to stare at the gypsy gyrating in a wheelchair.

"Excuse me… you there." Then she said it louder. "Excuse me!"

Margerie took off the headphones and looked up like a reprimanded five-year-old.

"Do you live here?" Korff asked as if it couldn't be true. "I mean do you actually live in this building?"

Pointing towards the only apartment on the lobby floor she answered a bit too cheerfully. "Oh yes, right there in L1."

"You mean you rent," she said disdainfully. "You're one of those Roth renters."

Turning around she scowled at Hector before moving on. "You should be standing by the door, it's what we pay you for. You're not here to socialize." That said, she turned towards the elevator and left a chastened doorman, garish cripple, and Celia Cruz, silenced in the lobby. Pushing a button, the door opened. When it closed, Brobit ascended to her penthouse.

82

Les Miserables

She couldn't keep track of Victor. After three months in Cincinnati, he took off for Albuquerque. Later she got postcards from Denver and Santa Fe. Nothing felt right so he went back to Chicago. Two years later he returned to Manhattan.

AIDS was rampant. Thousands of gay men in New York had died, and two of Victor's friends were on their way out. Familiar faces had abandoned empty bars and he had no idea where they all had gone.

Margerie welcomed him back with an invitation. Katie Summers planned on flying in for the opening of *Les Misérables*, but after something came up in Hollywood, sent the tickets to her aunt. When Vic arrived at his friend's new address, she was in a wheelchair talking to the doorman. Wearing a gold brocade stole and black velvet gloves, prosperity suited her. He gave his friend a hug and they left for the theater.

Settling into third-row aisle seats they noticed Mayor Koch sitting in front of them. During the second act he turned around to stare at whoever was crunching a carrot; Margerie waved and finished her snack. Three glorious hours flew by. Waiting for the theater to empty before wheeling her out, they both agreed the musical deserved a long run.

On the way back they stopped for a drink and their conversation shifted to what everyone was talking about. Over a glass of wine Margerie told him Broadway star Frank Rose committed suicide after an AIDS diagnosis and that Collie Berg, her director at The Actors Studio, died of the plague a week later. Victor didn't mention the boyfriend he'd lost last spring. Margerie liked Jorge, he'd save more sad news for another time. Reminiscing about their old neighborhood she said she'd seen Ray Ginetti in Macy's the week before Christmas. He looked terrible. On New Year's Day he made all the papers; ended it all by leaping off the Staten Island Ferry.

Vic heard too many stories from too many people. Everyone seemed to be compiling a list. What was the point? He ordered another drink. "It's intense," he said. "You'd think there'd be some hope."

Margerie reached over and touched his hand. "Be patient dear, things pass. Keep your spirit up."

Vic had something to say he thought she'd understand. "Now that I'm back I see names in the paper. People tell me about someone I knew, guys I slept with and people I cared about. You get to a point where you don't want to hear it but listen anyway." Victor lit a cigarette. "When we got to the theater, I saw all these happy people, dressed up and rushing in for a Broadway premiere. I was excited, glad to be with you doing something that only happens in New York. But when I looked up at the marquee I thought about Jacob, Mark, and Carlos. Guys who've died." Victor choked up. "It was there in blazing neon... my tribe, these men... Les Misérables."

83

Sometimes Japanese

Now seventy-five, exaggeration bonded with age. Anecdotes about stars she'd known, parts she'd played, and places she'd been, grew bigger than they were. Details blurred, settings changed, and nothing retold was ever the same. Rumors before, now became fact. Hazy recollections expanded. Margerie told stories that surprised her as much her audience.

Carrying an arsenal of vitamins and herbs, Margerie dispatched small bottles onto restaurant tables like tiny sentinels preparing for war. After years of restraint, her clothes got brighter. Pink or yellow scarves accented lime and aqua blouses; a red polka dot sweater got topped off with a turban that screamed mandarin orange. Embracing color, she was ready to roll.

Venturing out depended on her roommate's timetable. After Elaine got tickets for a Saturday matinee, she told Margerie she was going to a sale at Gimbels and would be back around noon. Preparing for an early curtain like an eight o'clock opening, she strategically applied foundation makeup. After that, she glued on long lashes, colored her eyelids turquoise, and penciled on narrow black eyebrows. To finish the look she was after, she powdered her face with "Alabaster Moon" then coated her lips Cardinal red. Even for theater people the effect was remarkable.

Ready and waiting time did not fly. Glancing in a mirror she powdered again and reapplied lipstick. By the time Elaine got home she'd refreshed her appearance several times.

After the final curtain she critiqued a disappointing second act as she got wheeled through the lobby. Navigating their way through the crowd Elaine noticed an astonished little boy pulling on his mother's sleeve.

"Look mom," he shouted, then pointed at the lady in the wheelchair. "Kabuki!"

Oblivious to it all Margerie chattered on, but Elaine had heard the precocious child. Later, preparing for bed, she told her friend the powder was too pallid. "Do you really think so?" she said, then smeared on cold cream. "Well, it is alabaster dear. A classic if you ask me. White can never be too white," she reasoned. "And you've got to admit, it brings out my eyes."

84

Order dessert

March roared in like a lion. Garbage strikes, wretched weather, and a pernicious flu chewed on the city; getting out of bed took courage. Rushing to work Elaine fought the elements. Preoccupied and determined her umbrella wouldn't turn inside out, she stepped in front of a skidding limousine. It barely touched her but slipping on a patch of ice, down she went. A traffic cop was about to call an ambulance when Elaine stood up and refused medical attention. After taking cards from the driver and policeman, she hailed a cab and went home to change clothes.

Elaine seemed more concerned about her coat and umbrella than anything else, but Margerie insisted she could've been killed. After looking at a gruesome bruise on her leg, one word came into both minds: lawsuit.

Four years since their settlement, better living had its price. Leaving furnished rentals behind they had to start from scratch. They needed a bed, convertible sofa, blankets, sheets, rugs, and towels. After that they got two Barcalounger chairs, 4 lamps, a coffee table, dressers, pots, pans, and plates; then bought a television and signed up for cable.

Overdue dental work cost thousands of dollars but was worth every penny. Elaine found a marvelous stylist to cut and color their hair and a fabulous nail salon was just around the corner. Taking a dream vacation, they boarded luxury liner QE2 for a trip to London. Margerie was wearing a new mink jacket, Elaine looked stunning in a cashmere coat. A year later they traveled first class on a train from Montreal to Vancouver. And they weren't selfish; at Christmas they handed out tips to all the service people and made a generous contribution to the Salvation Army. Everyone liked them. It was true: money changed everything.

Even so, Margerie's income was a meager social security check and Elaine's position as a management secretary had peaked. Time passed. Abby Roth raised their rent twice; $2100 a month was New York reasonable. With $33,000 left in the bank they refused to worry. Perhaps good fortune would call again.

By the time Elaine called the office a new option surrounded her impairment. Unfortunately, their beloved lawyer Gabe had moved to Boston. When someone at work said her cousin was a personal injury attorney, Elaine thought it was auspicious; got his number and called.

Abrasive, aggressive, and blunt, Warren Growski sounded like he knew what he was doing. He gave her the name of a doctor who'd get her on disability, said to buy a cane and make sure to use it. His fee was 35% of any settlement, but he wanted $2000 upfront for a research assistant. When asked what to expect Growski was optimistic. "Pain and suffering… two, three hundred thou at least." Then added assuredly, "Trust me. It's a piece of cake."

85

Sign it

It cost money to prove pain and suffering. Advised to stay on disability, Elaine's income was half of what it was. Charging ahead, Warren insisted she see another neurologist. After the doctor prescribed expensive painkillers, Growski told her to get frequent refills and save the receipts.

Eight months passed before negotiating with Atlas Mutual. In spite of a deposition from the cop plus a file of medical records it was a disaster. Because Elaine refused medical aid at the scene, the insurance giant challenged the claim and offered $4,000 to settle. Outraged, Growski insisted he 'had them by the balls' and was going to court. After asking Elaine for $2000 he needed for 'more clerical,' he told her 'easy street is right around the corner.'

Increased stress disabled Margerie; even taking a few steps hurt. Elaine made an appointment with a West Side chiropractor Broadway hoofers and popular athletes called Dr. Whiz. After waiting for three weeks, she had a 50-minute treatment and bought three bottles of a special formula. It cost them $495 but vitality failed to surge into her legs.

When Abby Roth sent another lease renewal raising rent to $2400, Elaine burst into tears. "Don't worry," Margerie sighed, "just sign it. What else can we do?" Their account at Chemical Bank had dwindled to $4301.24.

86

Daffodils

Born and raised in California, Katie Summers progressed from a teenage role on a television sitcom to an Academy Award. Watching her ascent from the East Coast, Margerie continued to send letters and cards but had only seen her niece six times in 30 years.

She never mentioned struggles, but Katie knew her life hadn't been easy. She loved her aunt but Hollywood made its own demands. Along with a busy career she had a husband, three children, six people on payroll, and positions on two charity boards.

Back on East Fifty-Fourth, anxiety intensified. Elaine's court date was delayed again, and they were late on rent. She'd never asked Katie for anything but now seventy- seven, wrote her niece and explained their predicament. Unable to pay bills, Margerie had no one else to ask.

Five days later the doorman delivered an Air Express envelope from Los Angeles. Inside on a card with yellow daffodils her niece had drawn a smiling face. "Hope this helps! Love, Katie." Enclosed was a check for $20,000.

87

It happened.

Whatever they needed cost more; their rent went up again. After two years of support, Katie wrote a letter suggesting they look for housing outside of Manhattan. Confined and unable to concentrate, Margerie depended completely on Elaine.

When the lawsuit finally got to court they were deeply in debt. The judgment was $6,000; thirty-five percent went to Growski. The 'piece of cake' their attorney promised didn't cover two months they owed in rent.

After Abby Roth ordered an eviction, a sheriff taped a notice on their front door. The next day they got a bill from Con Ed in an envelope with a red stripe: pay up or live in the dark. Desperate and depressed, their apartment was as disordered as they were. Magazines, plastic bags, and a variety of papers, covered the floor. Clothes were tossed on chairs and tables, laundry waited to be washed. The kitchen sink was clogged, dirty dishes and silverware stayed on the counter. They'd seen a mouse but were too humiliated to call the super. Everything was a mess.

Finally, it happened. Drained and defeated they surrendered. Elaine called her brother in Oklahoma; he arrived three days later with a U-Haul and loaded what he could onto a truck. Crying as Elaine wheeled her into the lobby, Hector bent down, kissed Margerie's cheek, then wiped a tear off her face and gave her his number at home. She promised to call, but knew she wouldn't. Hailing a cab Hector told the driver to take them to JFK. Two hours later they were flying to Tulsa.

88

Tulsa

Elaine's brother, his wife, and divorced daughter, lived in a barren subdivision ten miles outside of Tulsa. In a room shared with Elaine, all Margerie saw from the window was a yard of brown grass and an empty inflatable pool. In spite of the difficult arrangement, she tried being cheerful. Before long, detachment seemed easier.

A portly minister from Frontier Baptist dropped by to say that Jesus loved her. He said the Lord had brought her to a land of decent people, then with a hand on her shoulder, praised Glory and left. His drugstore after-shave lingered like noxious gas: two hours later Margerie lost consciousness.

Raced to the hospital she rallied the next day. Tired but lucid her room reeked of disinfectant. A television mounted on the wall was never off but didn't muffle two groaning roommates. Hoping she'd eat, a nurse left lime Jello, meat loaf and corn, waiting on a plastic tray. It looked like dated pop-art and Margerie turned her head away. Ignored, lunch waited anyway.

A young doctor, who called her Margret, administered a strong sedative then hurried off to complete his rounds. Escaping into dreams, Margerie joined a joyful review. She weeded the garden and drank lemonade with her parents in Jamestown, then sat at a table with Daniel Drake and Elaine at the Roseland Ballroom. Marianna was there, dancing too close with Mateo. Izaak Korczak looked young, was in a tuxedo, laughing with Max and Molly. Maric and Katie were with Hector and they started clapping, cheering her on. After swimming with Tony in Chautauqua Lake, he kissed her again. Then stolen by the wind on a summer night, she soared over Madison Square, Broadway, and the bright lights in Times Square.

It was 6 pm in Oklahoma; eight o'clock in New York. The curtain was about to go up at the Shubert. She recognized the scent of Elaine's favorite perfume, could hear crying, and knew she was holding her hand. But euphoria beckoned. Unwilling to resist, Margerie took a final breath. As her body disengaged, she had one last thought: it sure felt good to get out of Tulsa.

Author, NYC 1977

Brent Isgrig studied at The University of Iowa's writing program with Donald Justice and Marvin Bell. Eager to find where he belonged, he took off for California, Arizona, New Mexico, then headed for Boston and the east coast. After stepping off a bus in New York City, he'd found his place and stayed there for three extraordinary decades. Now living in Chicago, he is working on another book and a collection of poems.